MW01166909

BUT NOT FORTUITOUS

A CLINT WOLF NOVEL
(BOOK 16)

BY

BJ BOURG

WWW.BJBOURG.COM

TITLES BY BJ BOURG

LONDON CARTER MYSTERY SERIES

James 516

Proving Grounds

Silent Trigger

Bullet Drop

Elevation

Blood Rise

CLINT WOLF MYSTERY SERIES

But Not Forgotten

But Not Forgiven

But Not Forsaken

But Not Forever

But Not For Naught

But Not Forbidden

But Not Forlorn

But Not Formidable

But Not For Love

But Not Forborne

But Not Forewarned

But Not Foreboding

But Not Forespoken

But Not For Blood

But Not Foreknown

But Not Fortuitous

BUT NOT FORTUITOUS
A Clint Wolf Novel by BJ Bourg

This book is a work of fiction.
All names, characters, locations, and incidents are products of the
author's imagination, or have been used fictitiously.
Any resemblance to actual persons living or dead, locales, or events
is entirely coincidental.

Cover design by Christine Savoie of Bayou Cover Designs

PUBLISHED IN THE UNITED STATES OF AMERICA

Acknowledgments:

I would like to extend my sincerest thanks to Shelby Latino, a morning Meteorologist in New Orleans, for helping to make my job easier. Her daily forecasts—delivered with such passion and expert knowledge—have helped to shape the weather in my novels for years. Time is extremely important to a writer, and her work has saved me countless hours of research and plotting. For this, I am eternally grateful.

Additionally, her forecasts often include local Louisiana flavor, which is also important to a writer whose novels are set in the area. With her permission, one such nugget from a recent forecast can be found in the pages of this novel. I'll leave it to the reader to find and identify it.

The job of a Meteorologist is extremely important. Not only do they keep us informed, but they also keep us safe—and Shelby Latino is the very best at what she does.

CHAPTER 1

Monday, July 13th
Mechant Loup, Louisiana

"Dad said we'd better be home by midnight," Paulie McKenzie warned from where he sat in the darkness behind Zeke. The pirogue only made a whisper of a sound as it glided through the water. The older brother guided the narrow wooden watercraft through a canal that spilled out of Bayou Tail to the north.

"We've got plenty of time," Zeke called over his shoulder. "Like I told you, my buddy said there's catfish the size of sharks where we're going. Dad won't care how late we are if we bring one of those home. Besides, he had to go to bed early, so he'll never know if we're a few hours late."

"I don't know. I don't like it. I've got a weird feeling."

Zeke sighed and pulled his paddle from the water. He twisted around and looked at his brother. The pirogue rocked gently from the movement. "Don't worry. Everything'll be fine. I promise."

Even in the dim glow from the moonlight, Zeke could see that Paulie was scared—unreasonably so. This worried Zeke. Ever since they'd gone through their incident six years ago, Paulie had been different. He'd left a part of himself in that strange attic long ago, and Zeke didn't think he'd ever get it back.

"It's okay," Zeke said in a soothing voice. "We'll set some lines, pass them once, and then head home. We'll be back before midnight."

Paulie seemed to relax a little. He nodded and dipped his own paddle in the water. The two brothers continued down the canal, where both sides were lined with short trees and thick underbrush. It was darker along the narrow waterway, and Zeke had to squint to penetrate the darkness. There was no shine on the water in this area.

The boys paddled for about a mile before reaching a cut in the trees to the right. Zeke told Paulie they had made it and steered the pirogue through the opening. A thick tree branch smacked him in the face. It stung. He issued a warning to Paulie and felt the pirogue dip to the left as Paulie dodged the branch.

The Louisiana air was warm and Zeke had broken out in a sweat, so he stopped paddling to peel off his shirt.

"Where are we?" Paulie asked, his voice betraying his nervousness.

"We're somewhere behind North Project Road."

"Is this private property?"

"My buddy says it's abandoned and that's why the catfish are so big in here—there's no one to catch them." The lake was narrow and Zeke headed for the opposite bank, where the ground was reportedly solid and wooded. "My buddy's grandpa said the man who used to own this land died and his family don't live around here, so it's just wasting away."

"Maybe we should go back and get the flatboat," Paulie said nervously. "That way we could get away in a hurry if somebody sees us."

"That pass is too shallow for a motor." Zeke tried not to sound impatient. "I already told you that a thousand times."

Paulie didn't say anything more as they paddled across the calm water, and Zeke was just as happy. When they were young, Paulie had been the daredevil while he had been the more cautious one. Those days were long gone. He didn't know if he'd ever get his brother back, and that saddened him deeply.

Once the front of the pirogue brushed against the bank, he placed his paddle beside him and reached for the catfish line. He took one end and secured it to a low-hanging branch. He worked swiftly and silently and was about to push off from the bank when he heard voices through the trees. Paulie gasped and Zeke saw him drop low in the pirogue.

Zeke reached for his brother—whose shoulder was trembling—and whispered a warning for him to stay quiet. He then moved toward the front of the pirogue where he could be closer to the bank. He opened his mouth and cocked his head in an attempt to hear what was being said, but it was no use. There were at least two people out there, but they were too far away to hear what they were saying.

Leaning back toward Paulie, Zeke whispered, "Stay here. I'm going check it out."

Paulie's right hand shot up and latched onto Zeke's bare shoulder. "No!" he said in a hoarse whisper. "Please don't go!"

Zeke gently removed his brother's hand. "I won't be long. I just want to see what's going on and if it's safe to run our lines."

"Don't be long. Please…please hurry."

"I will." After making the promise, Zeke stood and walked deftly to the front of the pirogue and jumped to the shore. After tying the pirogue in place and glancing once at Paulie, he began making his way through the thick underbrush. He took about a dozen steps and suddenly broke through the underbrush and found himself in a patch of thin woodlands. He squatted and surveyed the area. The moon cast a ghostly hue around the area and he felt the hair stand up on the back of his neck.

Should I go back? He couldn't hear the voices anymore, so he figured they must've gone. He hesitated, but then decided to push forward just to be sure they were alone. He didn't want to be caught illegally fishing on private property, because his dad would kill them for sure. His dad had warned Zeke more than once not to get in trouble again or he wouldn't make it to his fifteenth birthday—and he planned to live forever.

Zeke continued picking his way forward, using his bare feet to feel for twigs and dried leaves. He walked through pickers from time to time, but it didn't faze him. The bottoms of his feet were calloused and hard. He could walk across hot concrete in the middle of a Louisiana summer day or through an oyster shell driveway without flinching. It wasn't like he'd set out to develop tough feet—it just happened naturally after years and years of running around with no shoes. This superpower came in handy often in the swamps.

After traveling about a hundred yards through the forest, he paused and listened. Nothing. He sighed in relief. It appeared they were now alone to fish for some giant catfish. He was just turning to head back toward the pirogue when a glint of light caught his eye. He froze in place and blinked. There it was again—just a twinkle of light, but evidence that they were not alone in these woods.

He hesitated, fear wrapping its icy hands around his chest and squeezing tightly. He considered turning and running back to the pirogue and high-tailing it out of there, but curiosity got the best of him. His heart beating like a war drum in his chest, he dropped to his knees and began crawling along the forest floor. He rose to his knees intermittently to make sure he was heading in the right direction.

Each time he did so, the glow from the light grew stronger.

Finally, after what seemed like forever, Zeke came upon a tiny clearing in the woods. He peeked around a tree and frowned at the scene before him. A shovel was stabbed upright into a mound of dirt at the far edge of the clearing. It was a few feet from a giant oak tree. A lantern hung from one of the branches. He didn't see anyone and he didn't hear a sound. Taking a deep breath and holding it, he stepped out from behind the tree and paused. Nothing happened. He took a step forward and still nothing happened.

Emboldened now, he walked directly to the mound of dirt. The earth had been recently turned—as best he could tell in the dim glow from the lantern—and the hole was empty. Something caught his eye at the innermost edge of the surrounding shadows. As he moved in that direction, he realized it was a leather satchel.

Buried treasure!

Zeke's excitement mounted as he rushed forward. Like everyone else in town, he had heard the rumors about an ancient treasure being buried near one of the lakes in Mechant Loup. Could this be the lake? Had someone found the treasure? If so, why would they leave it behind? He considered the possibility that there had been several bags in the hole and that maybe the treasure hunters had been forced to make multiple trips to their getaway vehicle. If so, they would be back for this one—but when? How much time did he have?

Zeke dropped to his knees beside the satchel and tore frantically at the straps, desperate to get it open and see what was inside. He groaned inwardly when he realized there were locks on the straps. He had a knife in his pocket, but the straps were made of thick leather. Realizing he had only one choice, he slung the satchel over his shoulder and turned to hurry back to the pirogue. As he stepped back into the glow from the lantern, he realized something was wrong, but he couldn't immediately put a finger on it.

He stood there frozen, inspecting every inch of the clearing. He hadn't heard as much as a whisper of a sound. For a brief moment, he wondered if he could have stumbled upon sacred ground and if the spirits of dead Native Americans had been awakened and angered. After all, this had once been the land of the Chitimacha Indians, and he had heard stories of their ghosts roaming the swamps seeking to reclaim their territory. He quickly dismissed the thought as ludicrous.

It was at that very moment he realized what was different about the clearing—the shovel was gone.

Realizing he had made a huge mistake, he whirled around to run in the opposite direction. He hadn't taken a single step when a bright light exploded violently inside his brain. His last cognizant thought was wondering if he had run into a tree. The bright light then shut off and everything cut to black.

CHAPTER 2

"What day is it?" I rubbed the sleep from my eyes and glanced around the room.

Susan sat up in bed and stretched, her breasts testing the fabric of her T-shirt. After a soulful yawn, she turned her brown eyes in my direction and shrugged. "Tuesday, I think."

We had gone to bed early last night and the night before that, but we hadn't done much sleeping. My mom and dad had taken Grace to Disney World for two weeks and they'd left on Sunday. We loved our two-year-old daughter more than we loved each other and we hadn't wanted her to leave, but we'd finally relented when we realized it might be good for her to spend some time with her grandparents. After all, they weren't getting any younger and my dad was always away for work, so they needed some quality time with their granddaughter—and I wasn't keen on kiddy theme parks anyway. I knew I'd eventually have to go to Disney World with Grace, but, for now, I'd been granted a reprieve.

Grace had only been gone an hour when Susan and I realized we were alone—totally alone—and could do whatever we wanted. We'd only put two things on the calendar for the week, and that was work and sex, but not necessarily in that order.

Like a man who'd been drugged, I reached for my cell phone and checked the display screen. "Do we have time for another conversation before work?"

We had begun referring to sex as a "conversation" about a month ago when we walked out of our bedroom to find Grace sitting on the floor just outside the door. In her broken English, she had asked what we were doing and Susan—whose face was burning with embarrassment at the time—had blurted, "Mommy and Daddy were having a conversation."

Susan was already in the bathroom and I could hear the motor from her toothbrush buzzing. She walked to the bathroom door and mumbled something I couldn't understand, but from the tone of her voice, I knew the odds weren't good for a conversation.

Sighing heavily, I pushed myself to my feet and joined her in the bathroom.

"What're your plans for the day?" I asked.

She rinsed her mouth and wiped it with a towel that hung from the rack. "Amy's friend from Tellico Plains will be here today. We'll be going down to the mayor's office to get her sworn in and then I'll show her around town."

Amy Cooke had been a patrol officer for the Mechant Loup Police Department until a few months ago, when Susan had agreed to let her go to work for me as a detective for the town. Amy had promised to help find her replacement and, true to her word, she had come through for us.

"Who is she?" I asked.

"Her name's Regan Steed. She's a ten-year veteran of law enforcement. She worked for the Tellico Plains Police Department before coming here."

I stepped into the shower and called out, "Amy told me her husband was transferred to this area for work."

"Yeah, he's some kind of supervisor at one of the big oil companies. I didn't get the name, but it's out of Lafayette."

"That's a long drive."

"They wanted to live close to the swamps and Amy spoke highly of our little town, so this is where they're deciding to call home."

"From one small town to the next," I mumbled, and finished my shower. Once I was dressed, I met Susan downstairs for breakfast. Achilles had slipped through the doggy door earlier—it was a big one, because he was a 100-pound German shepherd—and he now stuck his head through from the outside to see what was going on. I figured he must've smelled the sizzling bacon.

"You know you can't have table scraps," I said, glaring playfully at him. He cocked his head to the side, as though deciding if he should challenge me, but he quickly pulled away and ran off when Coco started barking at something in the back yard. While Achilles was solid black except for a little tan, Coco was a saddleback German shepherd and was a female. I'd rescued her from a bad situation a while back. She and Achilles had instantly fallen in love.

After watching the morning news while eating breakfast, I grabbed my holster and kissed Susan goodbye.

"I'm right behind you," she called.

I checked on the dogs. They had a large raccoon treed in the back yard. I chuckled and then headed for work in my unmarked Tahoe. We lived south of town, but the drive to the office was not a very long one, unless something happened to prolong the trip—and that's exactly what happened on this morning.

I had been traveling along Main Street and was approaching Mechant Groceries when an old beat-up truck came barreling down on me. As though they didn't know my black Tahoe was a police vehicle—or they didn't care—the vehicle swerved into the left lane and whisked past me. We were in a no-passing zone and I was going the speed limit.

I tried to see who was driving as it sped by, but the windows were tinted. I never did like enforcing traffic laws, but I figured the truck might end up killing someone, so I flipped the switch on my lights and activated my siren.

Snatching up my radio, I called dispatch and reported that I was attempting to pull over a red pickup truck traveling at a high rate of speed through the south side of town. Lindsey Savoie, our daytime dispatcher, came on and asked Officer Baylor Rice if he was available to respond.

"Ten-four," he said. "Where are you, Clint?"

"Approaching the old police department," I radioed. "It's not slowing down and we'll be out of town in a minute."

I backed off of the accelerator when I saw a car approaching Main Street from Washington Avenue. I just knew the car's driver wouldn't see the old truck and would pull right out in front of it, but, thankfully, I was wrong. Before reaching the Mechant Loup Bridge, which crossed over Bayou Tail and was our only connection to the rest of the world to the north, the taillights brightened and the truck swerved right onto Grace Street. Through the back windshield, I saw the man shift violently to his left. Somehow, he managed to maintain control of his vehicle and shot down Grace before turning left onto a side street.

As I might've guessed, he headed straight for the boat launch. What I didn't know was if he would crash the truck into the water or stop short. I also didn't know what would happen once he exited his vehicle, but I was about to find out.

Rocks and dust shot into the air as he brought his truck to a sliding halt. I veered left and braked hard, positioning the engine of the Tahoe between me and his truck. I shoved my door open and—hand on pistol—stepped out into the hot air.

It wasn't even eight o'clock yet and I felt as though I'd stepped into a furnace. I shouldn't have been surprised, because I had been warned early this morning by our local meteorologist. Not only was she informative and accurate in her forecasts, but she was also entertaining, and had categorized the feels-like forecast for this afternoon as "swamp booty." I had laughed when I'd heard the forecast, but I wasn't laughing now. While it was still early, we were well on our way to that level of torture.

"Show me your hands!" I hollered to the figure that had stepped out of the driver's door. A hot breeze had whisked the dust away and I immediately recognized Red McKenzie standing there looking angry. I knew Red. While he was a hothead, he wasn't a bad man. I relaxed and approached him. "What's wrong, Red?"

He turned toward me and I frowned. I'd seen that expression on his face once before, and it could only mean one thing. He shrugged his sagging shoulders and a look of utter despair fell over his face.

"I…it's happening again. My boys didn't come home last night. They're…they're missing."

CHAPTER 3

I didn't waste any time. I immediately called Lindsey and asked her to have Melvin Saltzman meet me at the boat launch with his boat. Melvin was a longtime Mechant Loup police officer and he was better on the water than anyone I knew. He usually worked the nightshift on patrol, but he always responded when we needed him.

Baylor pulled up a few seconds later and approached my Tahoe as I began questioning Red.

"They grew up on the water and I know they can take care of themselves," Red explained, "but I can't help but worry. They've always come home."

"Do they have a cell phone?"

He frowned. "I can't afford the service. Besides, the reception is spotty where we live. It doesn't pay to have one."

"What were their plans last night?"

"They were running catfish lines in Lake Berg—like they've been doing every night since summer started." He rubbed his face, as though trying to flatten the worry lines that had spider-webbed across his leather skin. "They're usually home when I get up at six, but their boat wasn't there when I woke up this morning. I figured that maybe they had a busy night and were just running late, so I made my coffee and waited on the wharf. It was about fifteen minutes ago when Brennan Boudreaux floated by the camp with a group of tourists. I asked if he'd been out to Lake Berg and he said he had. I asked if he saw Zeke and Paulie, but he said he hadn't. He said he saw an aluminum hull tied to a tree on the eastern bank of the lake, but no one was around it. He said he figured the operator had hiked into the marsh to fish."

I nodded, considering what he'd just said. Brennan Boudreaux—
the brother of former mayor Dexter Boudreaux—owned Brennan's
Seafood and Swamp Tours. The elderly man had spent most of his
life on the water and would recognize the signs if there was trouble
on the water.

"Is it possible the boat broke down and they hiked through the
marsh?"

Red nodded. "That's what I thought at first. They pull their
pirogue behind the aluminum hull in case they break down or in case
they need to get into shallow water, so that's why I came here. I
thought they might've paddled here, but…"

He allowed his voice to trail off and I nodded my understanding.
I could hear the fear in his voice. I turned to Baylor. "I'll jump in
with Melvin when he gets here and we'll check the lake. Can you
drive up and down along Bayou Tail Lane and Back Street and
search the banks of the bayou?"

Baylor nodded and hurried to his patrol car. Static scratched
across my radio and Melvin's voice came on to say he would be at
the boat launch in five minutes. As I watched Red pace back and
forth in the shells, I took a call from Susan and explained what was
going on. When I ended the call, I retrieved a notebook from my
vehicle and handed it to Red.

"Write down the names of your boys' friends. If you know their
numbers, write them down, too, as well as their parents' names,
numbers and addresses."

Red got busy. As he wrote, he explained he didn't know any of
their numbers except for one of the fathers. "We work together, so
that's how I know him. Zeke goes to school with his son. Bart's his
name. Other than that, I don't really know how to contact their
school friends. My boys spend all their time on the water. Hell, if I
didn't threaten them, they wouldn't go to school at all."

I remembered life as a young boy in Louisiana. We lived on the
edges of La Mort and, while I had access to the swamps, it was
nothing like the paradise in which Zeke and Paulie were growing up.
Had I been them, I would never have wanted to go to school either.

Red handed me the notebook and I began scanning it when
Melvin's F-250 came rumbling into the parking lot of the boat
launch. Amy also showed up in her marked Dodge Charger. I walked
away from Red and greeted her when she exited her vehicle.

"What can I do?" she asked, tugging at the waistline of her jeans.
Her blonde hair was pulled back in a ponytail and the top of her
blouse was open two buttons down. "I've dealt with these kids

before. When I was on patrol, I was always getting complaints about them trespassing on private land. I caught them a few times. Usually, they were just hunting or fishing where they weren't wanted—nothing serious."

I ripped out the sheet of names and handed it to her. "Can you run down their friends while I run to the lake with Melvin? A flat boat was seen on the northern end of the lake, so it might be theirs."

She scanned the list, nodding as she did so. "I'll find out when they last spoke to Zeke and Paulie and if the boys had any plans that deviated from their normal activities."

"Sounds good." I glanced over at Red, who was helping Melvin launch the department's boat. "Also, press the kids to see if Zeke and Paulie were involved in anything criminal. Maybe they did something stupid and got into trouble."

Once she was gone, I grabbed my shotgun and joined Melvin. Red glanced at my shotgun and raised an eyebrow. "Are we expecting trouble?"

"We're just being cautious," I explained. I shot a thumb toward the boat. "You're welcome to join us."

He nodded and quickly boarded the vessel. Once we were all onboard, Melvin fired up the engine, backed away from the dock, and headed for the lake. It was still hot, but the wind offered a bit of comfort as we raced westward along Bayou Tail. I scanned both banks and the surface of the water as we rode, hoping to catch a glimpse of the boys or their pirogue. We weren't positive the boat that Brennan Boudreaux had seen belonged to the McKenzie brothers, but the chances were high that it did.

We traveled westward for about a mile until we reached the mouth of the lake. Melvin leaned over and removed his binoculars from a hatch and handed them to me. I began scanning the lake as we headed north. I had to close one eye to better focus on the lake, but nothing stood out as suspicious.

Melvin had slowed the boat significantly so that he and Red could scan the tree line to the east. I continued searching the waters to our west, but I came up empty. We had traveled a little over a mile when Melvin called out that he saw the aluminum hull that Brennan Boudreaux had reported. I moved to the starboard side of the boat and leaned out over the water so I could see where he was pointing. The spray from the boat felt good against my face, but it was so hot that the droplets almost dried in mid-air.

"I see it!" Red called from beside me. "That's their boat!"

Red was a big man and I had to stretch a little farther out to see around him, but I finally saw the flatboat tied to a tree branch on the eastern bank of the lake. Melvin pulled back on the throttle and the boat slowed even more. The boat was positioned in a shadowy area of the bank where the trees hung low over the water. I squinted to pierce the deep shadows as we coasted toward the boat. When we came to within a foot of it, Red reached out and grabbed onto the side.

"It's empty." His voice seemed to sink a little. "And their pirogue is gone."

Melvin pointed to a break in the bank. "This opens into a little canal that spills into a private lake. It's shallow until you reach the middle, so we'll have to use the push poles to get through this cut and the shallow parts. The boys probably took the pirogue to explore the lake, because they would've definitely buried their motor."

"A private lake?" Red asked.

Melvin nodded. "I've been called out here a few times to run people off, but I haven't been here in at least ten years. I think the original owner died. I don't know who owns the property now."

"Damn it!" Red pushed a bead of sweat from his forehead. "I told them boys to stay off of private property. I'm tired of having people complain about them trespassing."

"It's hard to know that it's private," Melvin explained. "There're no signs to keep people out, so I've never issued citations for trespassing. I would just inform them—it was mostly kayakers—that it's private and I'd never see them in the area again."

"But I told them a thousand times, if they're not positive it's public land, to stay the hell out."

"It's okay," I said, putting a hand on his shoulder. "Let's just focus on finding them. Once we know they're safe, then you can then get mad at them."

He grumbled, but nodded his agreement.

CHAPTER 4

Melvin and I began using the push poles to get the department boat through the shallow portion and into the deeper water of the private lake. It was no easy task and it took us a little over an hour. Once we'd made it, Melvin fired up the engine and began making the round of the perimeter. We hadn't gone far when I saw Melvin put his right hand to his forehead to shield his eyes.

"Look," he said, pointing across the lake. "I see something under that tree."

"That's it!" Red hollered in excitement. "That's their pirogue!"

I had to grab onto the side of the boat as Melvin jerked the steering wheel in that direction. The motor roared as it carried us across the narrow waterway. As we drew nearer, it seemed obvious that the pirogue was empty. I glanced at Red. His face had lost its color and his shoulders slumped.

"Dear God," he whispered, "please let my boys be okay."

My heart began to thump in my chest and I said a silent prayer myself. Red's boys were mischievous and adventurous, but they were good kids—and they were his life. If something had indeed happened to them, I didn't know if we would be able to control Red's outburst without hurting him. I was hoping it wouldn't come to that.

"I'm turning up mud," Melvin said. He shut off the engine and activated the switch that raised the motor. We glided forward, still a dozen yards from the pirogue.

Still holding on to my push pole, I set it in the water and gave it a shove. "Come on, please be okay," I whispered, staring intently toward the pirogue. I was hoping for a sign or a clue—anything to indicate that everything was okay and that the boys had simply gotten lost or stranded out here.

We had almost reached the pirogue when I heard branches snapping somewhere to the right and off in the trees.

"Zeke!" Red hollered. "Paulie! Where are y'all?"

The thick underbrush directly across from the pirogue began rustling loudly, as though a fight was taking place within the bushes, and then Paulie was standing there. He looked a mess. He wore dirty jean shorts, a torn T-shirt, and there was another shirt wrapped around his head. His face and arms were covered in welts, mud, and scratches.

"He's gone, Dad," the twelve-year-old boy said. "I can't find him anywhere."

Without waiting for us to reach the shore, Red launched himself out of the boat and into the waist-deep water. He waded toward his son, demanding to know what was going on.

"Zeke...Zeke wanted to fish for some big catfish," Paulie explained tearfully. "And then we heard people talking in the woods. Zeke went to go see who it was and—"

"You mean he left you here all alone?" Red demanded.

Paulie nodded his head. "I begged him not to go, but he wanted to make sure everything was safe. He didn't come back. He just disappeared. I can't find him anywhere. I mean, I didn't go far because I was scared, but I can't find him."

Melvin and I had pushed the boat up against the shore and we both jumped to the bank. I stood patiently by while Red continued to question Paulie—it was more like a hostile interrogation. I wanted to interject, but dared not for fear of setting Red off. I needed the man to stay as calm as possible so we could figure out what happened out here and locate Zeke.

"What in the hell are y'all doing here in the first place?"

"I told you, Dad, Zeke wanted to catch some giant catfish. His buddy from school said they had the biggest fish in this lake."

"Which buddy? That kid, Bart?"

Paulie nodded.

Red lifted his head and scanned the forest to the east, and I did the same. Beyond the trees, about a mile away, was Westway Canal. On the other side of the canal was a neighborhood. Had Zeke gotten lost and made it to the neighborhood? There were a few wooden bridges at various spots along the canal, and I remembered there being one near a pumping station somewhere east of us.

"Should we get a chopper in the air?" Melvin asked me out of the corner of his mouth.

I considered the idea. If Zeke was lost in the trees, we would most likely not be able to see him from the sky. Additionally, he might be simply goofing off, and I certainly didn't want to waste the pilot's time or fuel unless we were sure we needed him.

"Let's give it a minute," I said.

"How long ago did Zeke leave to find these people?" Red wanted to know from Paulie.

He shrugged. "It was last night. A long time ago. We came straight here from home. We were about to set out the lines when we heard the voices."

"He's been gone all night and you never thought to get help?" Red's voice was loud and threatening. "What in the hell is wrong with you, son?"

Tears streamed down Paulie's face. "I was scared, Dad. I was just too scared to move."

I stepped forward and put an arm around Paulie's shoulders, facing Red as I did so. "That's enough, Red. I'll take it from here."

I didn't want to have to put the man down in front of his kid and under these circumstances, but I wasn't going to let him take his frustrations out on Paulie.

Red took a breath and averted his gaze. I thought I saw a tear leak from his left eye. "Okay," he said softly. "I'm sorry. I'm just really scared right now."

"It's okay," I said, turning away from Red and kneeling in front of Paulie. "Okay, son, you said you last saw Zeke sometime last night. What time did you leave your house?"

"It had just gotten dark—"

"They left around nine o'clock," Red interjected. "That's what time they always leave to run their catfish lines. They're expected home by midnight. They usually wake me up when they get back so I can know they're safe. I didn't realize they hadn't come home until I woke up this morning. I guess I just slept through the night."

Red's voice was laced with guilt. I asked Paulie if he had heard any noises after Zeke left.

"I thought I heard some people talking, but they weren't talking as loud as when we first heard them. And then I heard somebody walking around in the woods. They got close to here and I got scared. I...I hid in the bushes." He pointed to his face. "The mosquitoes were really bad, so I wrapped Zeke's shirt around my face and crawled into a hollowed-out tree. I...I stayed there all night until I heard your boat motor coming." His chin started quivering as he looked past me at his dad. "I knew my dad was coming to save us, and I know you'll find Zeke—won't you, Dad?"

Red brushed by me and dropped to his knees. He wrapped Paulie in his bearlike arms. "Yeah, I'll find Zeke, Paulie. I'll find him and bring him home and y'all are never going to scare me like this again."

I glanced over at Melvin and indicated the woods. "Can you start a track?"

He nodded his bald head and disappeared into the brush. For as large and strong a man as he was, he was deceptively light on his feet. Not a leaf crackled nor a branch snapped as he began working to pick up Zeke's trail in the woods.

I directed my attention back to Paulie. "Son, can you tell me anything at all about the voices you heard? Did they sound old or young?"

"Um, I don't know."

"Male or female?"

"I…I think they were men."

"How many of them do you think there were?"

"I guess one or two."

"Did they have an accent? Did they sound local?"

"I really didn't hear their voices that good." He took a shivering breath. "I was too scared to pay attention. I don't really know what happened. I just want to find Zeke and go home."

I frowned and nodded. I was about to ask another question when my police radio scratched to life. It was Melvin and his voice was serious. "Clint, you need to see this."

Red jumped to his feet. "I'm coming with you."

"No, you need to stay here with Paulie." He opened his mouth to object, but I lifted a hand to silence him. "Your son needs you. He was abandoned once and look what happened, so don't you dare leave his side—got it?"

Our eyes locked for a long moment, but I guess he realized I wasn't in the mood to play around. He finally sighed and nodded. "Okay, I'll stay here with Paulie. Just please bring back Zeke."

CHAPTER 5

Police Chief Susan Wolf had monitored her radio from the moment she'd left her house earlier in the morning until she had reached the police department. Clint had stopped a speeding truck at the boat launch and then he'd called for Melvin to get a boat in the water. After a brief call with Clint, she'd learned that two boys were missing. She had considered heading in that direction, but Regan Steed was waiting for her at the office and it would be rude for her to be late on their first meeting.

After their initial greetings, Susan had taken Regan to the town hall to be sworn in by Mayor Pauline Cain. Regan's husband had to work, so the only people attending the small ceremony were Susan, Pauline, Pauline's staff, police officer Takecia Gayle, and three of the town council members. Once it was over and they'd had refreshments, Susan and Regan left the town hall and returned to the police department.

"We'll need to order you some uniforms," Susan said after she'd given Regan a tour of the building and they were seated in her office. "Do you know your sizes?"

"Thankfully, I recorded the sizes of my uniforms from Tellico Plains PD." She dug out her cell phone and called out some measurements. When she was done, she grunted. "When I first started working in law enforcement, they were issuing men's uniform pants to women officers. Have you tried those?"

Susan grinned knowingly and nodded, remembering her early days as a police officer. "Our curves were not meant to be squeezed into man pants."

"Exactly!" When Regan smiled, her hazel eyes sparkled. "I was dating my husband at the time and he made this God-awful face when I modeled my uniform for him. I was proud of myself. I thought I looked good in uniform. When I asked him what was wrong, he told me to turn around again. I did and he said that my top half was all woman, but my bottom half looked like a man. I went to my bedroom and checked out my ass in the full-length mirror and he was right!"

"What'd you do?"

"I tore those things off and immediately returned them to the police department. I told the chief if he didn't find me a set of women's pants, I would be wearing Daisy Dukes and a gun belt to work." She leaned back in her chair and grinned again. "He got on the phone to Gall's and ordered five women's uniform pants right quick."

Susan laughed and was about to pull up the Gall's website when Lindsey hollered from down the hall. "Chief! There's a fight at Mitch Taylor's Corner Pub!"

Without a moment's hesitation, Susan was on her feet. "Let's go!"

Regan was almost as fast as Susan. Her five-foot, five-inch frame moved with lightning speed as she followed Susan down the hallway and through the lobby. Before they reached the front door, Susan put on her sunglasses and she told Regan to do the same. She knew the barroom would be dark and she wanted her pupils to be dilated when she entered the establishment. If the fight was still taking place, she wouldn't have time to allow her eyes to adjust to the darkness, so the sunglasses would help to give her a little edge.

"It's four blocks down," Susan called over her shoulder as she rushed down the large concrete steps of the building. "It's faster on foot!"

Susan's muscular legs stretched the fabric of her tan uniform pants as she raced up Washington Avenue. She grinned inwardly. She had taken a brutal beating months ago and, after an annoying stint in the hospital, had made a slow and frustrating recovery. But now, she felt good. She was back to her normal self and able to give it her all. She could hear Regan's boots pounding the concrete behind her and she felt good about her selection. There had been no hesitation in Regan when Susan announced the fight down the street, and she was keeping up just fine.

It was July in Mechant Loup and tourism was at an all-time high, making for crowded streets. After zigzagging in, out, and through the herd of people milling along the sidewalks, they finally reached the saloon.

Susan rushed through the door and immediately ripped off her sunglasses. She was just in time to see a bar stool go sailing across the room, having been launched by a big Cajun with tree trunks for arms and a busted nose. The target of the attack, a man of similar stature, batted the barstool away and snatched up a full bottle of beer as a weapon.

"Police! Break it up!" Susan hollered, heading straight for the big Cajun. Regan went for the man wielding the beer bottle. The Cajun, obviously inebriated, didn't give a second thought to the fact that Susan was a police officer. He reared back with his right arm and was intent on swinging his fist right at Susan's face, but the two never met. Instead, Susan sidestepped to the left and shot her right arm under the man's armpit and around the left side of his neck. Bringing her left hand up to meet her right hand, she clamped down like a python, executing a lateral vascular neck restraint that would've taken down a horse.

As she squeezed, Susan glanced in Regan's direction to see how she was faring. The man with the beer bottle had wrapped his arms around Regan in a bear hug and lifted her into the air. Regan's small frame had been completely enveloped by the man and Susan could no longer see her.

Susan scanned the crowd of people inside the establishment. Everyone had backed away from the fight and most of them were watching with excitement, while some turned away from the violence.

While it didn't appear the customers would interfere, it also didn't appear they would intercede on Regan's behalf. Susan was about to let go of her hold to help Regan when she saw the man's head snap back. His arms fell to his side. Suddenly, Regan's face came into view. Blood dripped down her forehead and her face was twisted in determination. She kicked the inside of the man's right leg and he fell to one knee. When she spun him around, Susan saw that the man's nose was flat and bloodied.

"I give up," the Cajun called right at that moment. His voice was fading. "I'm sorry for fighting. It's over. I...I quit."

Nodding, Susan released her grip and told the man to put his hands behind his back. When he did, she cuffed him and then tossed Regan an extra pair of handcuffs.

Once the two men were secured, Susan and Regan walked them outside and were set to parade them down the street to the police department when Baylor Rice's patrol car screeched to a halt on the street beside them.

"What the hell, Chief?" he asked, shaking his head at Susan. "I got here as fast as I could drive. How'd you beat me here on foot?"

Susan shrugged and led her prisoner to the back seat of his car. The man was so large it was difficult to squeeze him inside, but she finally managed to get him seated. Once Regan had placed her prisoner into the opposite side of the police car, Susan waved her over to the sidewalk and examined her forehead.

"You split your head pretty good," Susan commented. "You might need stitches."

Regan grinned. "It wouldn't be the first time."

Baylor dug out his first aid kit and retrieved a sterile trauma dressing packet. He handed it to Regan and she began cleaning off her face.

"Welcome to Mechant Loup," Susan said, slapping Regan's back. "I hope this didn't discourage you."

"Discourage me?" Regan grinned widely, exposing a row of perfect teeth. "Hell, this is my kind of town."

CHAPTER 6

I picked my way carefully through the woods, guided by Melvin's voice over the police radio. One of the best man trackers in the tri-parish area, Melvin was as comfortable in the woods as he was in his own living room. He also had the memory of a dolphin, and he was able to recall every piece of sign he'd located upon leaving the spot where we'd found Paulie.

"After a few more steps," Melvin said over the radio, "you're going to reach a cypress tree with a cypress knee shaped like a peace sign. Just to the right of that knee is a bare foot print. I think it belongs to Zeke. Once you reach that point, look straight ahead and you'll see where the trees start thinning out. I'm in that area."

Although he couldn't see me, I nodded and pushed forward until I reached the peace sign. I then looked up and, in the distance, I could see Melvin waving.

"If you walk straight toward me," Melvin said, "you won't disturb any sign."

I headed in his direction, but, as was my habit, I studied the ground as I walked. He was right. I didn't detect a single piece of evidence that any humans had been through there. I did see a deer track and those of a raccoon, but that was it. When I reached him, I glanced around. "What'd you find?"

Melvin pointed toward a large windthrown tree that was blanketed in moss. "Someone hid a shovel under that tree, and there's blood on it."

I frowned. "Fresh blood?"

"It's dry, but barely."

I moved beside Melvin and he guided my steps toward the

shovel. When we reached the spot, I looked down and still couldn't see it. "Where is it?"

"You've got to get on your hands and knees to see it."

I did as he suggested and had to nearly press my face against the forest floor to see into the narrow space under the fallen tree. I could smell the damp earth beneath me and feel the moisture seeping through the knees of my jeans.

Melvin aimed the beam of his flashlight at the shovel and I was able to see the blade. There were clumps of mud stuck to it, but I didn't see any blood. I then followed the light up the shovel to the handle and saw blood smeared up and down the wooden handle. It was definitely fresh.

I pushed myself up and glanced over at Melvin. "How in the hell did you find this?"

"I found a boot print in the soft mud that was headed in this direction," he explained simply. "I followed the sign to where it stopped on the other side of this tree trunk. I knew the person had to have come here for a reason, so I began searching every inch of this area. That's when I found the bloody shovel."

"Damn. I wonder whose blood it is."

Melvin pinched his eyes to clear the sweat from them. "Do you think it's the kid's?"

"I sure hope not." I pulled out my cell phone and photographed the shovel and the tree. "Where does the track come from?"

Melvin shot a thumb toward the northeast. "The person who made the tracks came from that direction. I intercepted the trail somewhere in the middle and followed it here. I wanted you to see the shovel before I continued in the opposite direction."

"Okay, I'm coming with you." I stood to my feet. "But first let me call Amy. I need her out here."

Amy answered on the first ring and immediately began talking. "Hey, Clint, I know where the boys were heading. One of Zeke's friends said they were looking for large catfish in this private lake behind—"

"North Project Road—and the friend's name is Bart."

There was a brief pause, and then, "How in the hell did you know that?"

"We found Paulie. He's safe, but Zeke's still missing." I told her about the bloody shovel. "I need you to get out here as quickly as you can. Take along some bolt cutters in case you need to cut the locks on the wooden bridge. Oh, and have Baylor follow you. I'll need your help processing this entire area, and I'll need Baylor to transport Red and Paulie to the station."

"What about Zeke?"

"I pray to God we find him unharmed, but I'm not feeling very optimistic at the moment."

After promising to be there in ten minutes, she ended the call. I drew my pistol and looked over at Melvin. "Let's do this."

I stood a little behind Melvin and slightly to his right. Holding my pistol in a two-handed ready grip, I scanned the area in front of us, to the left, and to the right. Occasionally, I checked our backside and I always searched the trees above us. It was my job to provide cover so he could devote his full attention to searching for "sign". He was relying on me to keep him safe, and I planned on doing just that.

The going was painstakingly slow. Melvin would stand in one spot for minutes at a time, studying the ground at his feet and the surrounding tree trunks and branches. He pointed out a flattened dry leaf in one spot. Several feet farther, he located a snapped branch. Farther still, he found a tiny piece of fabric snagged to the branch of a tree.

"We'll need to come back for this," he whispered, pointing at the fabric.

I nodded and took a picture of the tree and then a close-up of the fabric.

We had traveled about fifty yards from the windthrown tree when he stopped abruptly. I was paying attention to his every move, so I wasn't caught off guard. I also stopped and waited, wondering what he had seen.

After about two long minutes, he waved for me to move beside him. He pointed to the ground several feet away. "The ground in that area—it's been turned over recently."

My heart sank. There was a patch of earth roughly four feet wide and six feet long that appeared to stand out from the surrounding area. While it had been packed and smoothened in an attempt to make it blend in with the terrain around it, there were some subtle differences. In one spot, there was a blade of cut grass protruding from a clump of mud. A torn root was partially buried in another spot. There were a few other differences that Melvin pointed out.

"I hate to say this," he said, "but this is a grave."

I cursed under my breath and jerked out my phone to call Amy. When she answered, I asked her to bring some shovels.

"Oh, no," she said. "Did you find a buried body?"

"I sure hope not."

CHAPTER 7

"What's your name, Big Fella?" Susan asked the large Cajun who sat across the desk from her in the booking room.

"Joseph Billiot."

Susan jotted down his name. "Give me your age, date of birth, social security number, home address, and telephone number, please."

The man's large head was lowered as he provided the information. He had to ask her to repeat some of her questions, but she managed to get everything she needed for her report.

"I'm sure sorry I took a swing at you, Chief," he mumbled after a while. "I didn't realize you were a cop at the time."

"A hell of a way to find out." Susan was grinning, and that brought a smile from the older man. She noticed his right front tooth was missing, and she was certain that tooth had been the victim of some other barroom brawl. "So, what was the fight about?"

"Two guys from out of town came in to have a drink and they sat at the bar next to me. We got to talking and they seemed cool. They were interested in our culture—asked a lot of questions about alligators and fishing." Joseph rubbed a beefy hand across his face. "That other dude—the one I was fighting with—he was from New Orleans and he was acting the ass. He started saying if they wanted to see real Louisiana culture, they needed to go to New Orleans. He started putting us down. Saying we were backwater. One of the guys—the younger one—said he was from a small town, too—you know, defending me—and he said he didn't like cities. The New Orleans smartass called the man a little backwater bitch. The man called the smartass an asshole, and that's when the smartass from

New Orleans pushed him into his friend. They both spilled their drinks—they had mixed drinks—and one of the glasses fell to the floor and broke. The young guy wanted to fight the asshole from New Orleans, but the other man—he was pretty old, maybe seventy—pulled the younger guy back and told him to settle down. The young man grumbled about it, but then he paid for their drinks and my drink. He then left a tip for the bartender and they left."

"Did you get their names?"

"Ah, they said it earlier in the conversation, but I don't remember." He paused to rub the flesh where the handcuffs had dug into his wrists. "Anyway, I didn't like how the smartass from New Orleans came into our town and started running off the tourists, so I hit him."

"You hit him first?" Susan arched an eyebrow. "You were the aggressor?"

"Well, it was actually a push, but I knocked him right out of the saddle. He fell off that barstool like a sack of oysters hitting the dock. He looked shocked, like nobody had ever attacked him before. Me, I went back to my stool and sat down. It was over, as far as I was concerned. He pushed them, I pushed him—even Steven. That's when the smartass grabbed an empty bottle and threw it at me. Hit me right in the nose." Joseph pointed to the cut above the bridge of his nose. "Well, if he didn't want it to be over, then I wasn't finished with him. So, I grabbed the barstool and threw it at him. And then you showed up and tried to put me to sleep."

"In response to you throwing a punch at me," Susan corrected.

Joseph bowed his head sheepishly. "I'm real sorry about that. I didn't notice the uniform in the light from the door. It blinded me. I thought you were with him."

"I yelled police when I came through the door," Susan explained. "Didn't you hear me say that?"

"No, ma'am. I'm sorry."

"It's okay." Susan slid her notebook aside and grabbed a summons book from the drawer. "I'm going to ignore your attack on me and issue you a summons for disturbing the peace. If you pay your fine within thirty days, you can avoid going to court."

Joseph let out a long sigh of relief. "Thank you so much, Chief!"

"Don't mention it." Susan completed the misdemeanor summons, had Joseph sign it, and then handed him the hard copy. "Do you need a ride home? I think it's best if you don't go back to Mitch's place today."

"Yes, ma'am."

"You do need a ride?"

"Oh, no. I'll call my wife."

Once he was sitting in the lobby waiting for his wife, Susan walked to the holding cells in the back of the police department and glanced inside. The man from New Orleans was lying on his back in a bunk. He had a towel pressed against his face and he was moaning in pain. Susan shook her head. Regan hadn't made a sound when she'd head-butted the man, nor did she complain afterword.

Susan opened the cell door. "Let's go."

The man sat up and glared over the top of the towel. "Where are we going?"

"I'll take your statement and then—"

"I ain't saying shit to any of you backwater bitches!" The man spat the words. "I want my phone call. My lawyer will be down here so fast it'll blow the siding right off of the shit houses in this stink town!"

"If you hate this place so much, why are you here?"

"I work in the Gulf, so I have to pass through here." He grunted. "I just wish I would've never stopped."

"I understand." Susan stepped into the cell and sat on the bunk opposite the man. "Look, I just need your statement for the record and then I'll issue you a summons for disturbing the peace. I've already spoken to my officer, and she said she doesn't want to press charges against you for battery on a police officer. She said you got the worst of the ordeal."

"I didn't even know she was a cop," he grumbled. "She was wearing blue jeans and a shirt. I thought she was the bartender grabbing on me and I didn't appreciate it. I respect the law. I ain't like those young punks running around hating on cops. I never would've touched her if I would've known she was a cop."

"Did you hear me yell police as we came through the door?"

"I heard you say something, but there was so much confusion..."

His voice trailed off and Susan nodded. "What's your name?"

"George."

"Okay, George, what happened in there?"

"So, these two men come in from out of town and they started commenting about how beautiful the town is and how it's right in the middle of the swamps. They're just talking amongst themselves and this asshole—"

"His name is Joseph."

"Okay, *Joseph* interjected himself into their conversation and started acting like he was the Crocodile Dundee of the swamps. He was telling them bullshit stories about how he wrestles alligators for a living and catches cottonmouths with his bare hands." He shrugged. "It just got the best of me and I told them he was full of shit. Well, one of the men insulted me, so I might've shoved him a little."

"You pushed him?"

"Yeah, kinda. He fell into the other man that was with him and one of them dropped their drink." He shrugged again, as though it was no big deal. "That was it as far as I was concerned, but then they paid for their drinks and they gave *Joseph*"—he accentuated the name—"a $100 bill. I thought it was odd, but I couldn't hear what they told him, so I ignored it. They left and, next thing I know, I'm on the ground. This *Joseph* knocked me right off of my barstool, and I believe he was paid to do it."

Susan cocked her head to the side. "You think they paid him to avenge them?"

"Yes, ma'am."

"Wait here." Susan stood and walked out of the cell, down the hall, and into the lobby, where Joseph was still waiting for his wife. Susan walked directly to him and stood over him looking down. He shifted nervously in his chair and avoided making eye contact with her.

"What's up, Chief?"

"How much money did those strangers pay you to exact revenge on New Orleans?"

Joseph squirmed and laughed nervously. "What're you talking about?"

"You know damn well what I'm talking about." Susan held out her hand. "Fork it over."

Still refusing to look up at her, Joseph shoved a beefy hand into his pocket and pulled out a crisp $100 bill.

"Follow me," Susan said. "I'm adding a charge of simple battery to your summons. You can still pay it and avoid court, but don't ever do that kind of shit in town again. Understand?"

"Yes, ma'am," Joseph mumbled, shoulders drooping like a child who had been chewed out by his parents.

CHAPTER 8

It was noon before we started digging. Since we didn't know who owned the property and there was no such thing as a murder exception to the Fourth Amendment, I had called a judge and obtained a warrant to search the property for Zeke's body. While I didn't want to think he was dead and I wasn't about to share my thoughts with Red, I did have a horrible feeling in the pit of my stomach.

After obtaining the verbal search warrant, we'd somehow convinced Red to take Paulie and leave with Baylor, so he could take care of his younger son. He had demanded to know what we'd found in the forest, but I'd only told him we were still looking and for him to keep praying. He had glared suspiciously at me, but Paulie had begged to be taken home and away from the area. The young boy was clearly spooked. Baylor and I had walked them through the woods to where Baylor's cruiser was parked on our side of Westway Canal along a headland. Across the canal from the headland was a neighborhood that was situated just south of North Project Road.

When I'd returned to the fresh dig site, Amy had just finished taking pictures and Melvin was still searching the woods for Zeke. He had returned thirty minutes later to say there was no way Zeke was anywhere but inside that hole.

"The suspects—it looks like there were two of them—headed north. I followed the trail for a few hundred yards. They're long gone. I left a marker so I can pick up the track later. I figured my time would be better spent helping you dig."

"Is it possible one of the people you tracked was Zeke?"

Melvin frowned and shook his head. "Zeke's trail ends right here, and I'm afraid so does his life." He indicated the grave. "How're we going to do this?"

"Very carefully." I indicated the camcorder hanging around Amy's neck. "You ready to document it?"

Amy nodded and set the camcorder up on a tripod and began filming. After stating the date, time, location, and our reason for being there, the three of us began carefully digging. We scraped at the ground and removed an inch of dirt at a time. Since the dig was fresh, it was easy to remove the dirt and, within an hour, we had cleared out eighteen inches of earth.

My arms ached and my wet shirt clung to my body. Melvin had taken off his outer shirt and wrapped it around his head. Amy had stripped down to her tank top. We were all covered in mud, but the mud was a minor issue. The heat and humidity were such that it felt as though we were being waterboarded while we worked.

We were still digging when my radio, which was resting against a tree several feet away from me, scratched to life and Susan's voice came across the speaker.

"Clint, I'm approaching your location from the east. I've got food and water."

Collectively, we all sank back on our haunches and sighed. My stomach had been growling for two hours, and I knew Amy and Melvin had to be hungry, too. Like an angel appearing from out of the clouds, Susan broke from the thicker woods to the east and picked her way across the thinner woodlands surrounding us. A woman was with her, and I figured it was the new officer, Regan Steed. I wiped my sweaty brow and indicated the white bandage above Regan's eyebrow.

"What happened to you?"

She grinned, pointing to the bandage. "Twelve stitches. Apparently, Cajuns have hard heads."

"You should see the other guy," Susan said, as she picked a clear spot on the ground several yards away. She began removing individually wrapped Po-boys from a larger bag while Regan removed bottles of water.

I pulled myself to my feet and groaned when my knees popped loudly. I had just celebrated my thirty-sixth birthday last week, but I felt so much older than my actual age. "Damn, I'm getting old."

"I'll never get old," Amy said, as she reached for a Po-boy and took a seat against a nearby tree. "I'll die young."

I took a bite of my food and shook my head at her comment. After I swallowed, I said, "You don't have permission to die young. I need you."

While Melvin, Amy, and I wolfed down our food, Susan and Regan took up shovels and began scraping away the next layer of dirt. We then began taking turns digging. We moved faster working in shifts, and the earth began to recede at an even and quicker pace. It was an hour later when Amy called out that she found something. Melvin and Susan were also in the grave at the time, and they both stopped what they were doing to watch. I moved the tripod with the camcorder closer, and Regan and I gathered around to watch.

As sweat dripped from her tanned face, Amy blew a lock of blonde hair away from her eyes and dug gingerly with her fingers. Slowly, a bare torso started to come into view. I had been squatting beside the grave, but I sat down hard on my heels when Zeke McKenzie's face was unearthed.

"Poor kid," I mumbled, scanning the ominous trees surrounding us. "Who in the hell did this?"

Although I asked the question out loud, no one ventured an answer. We'd been asking ourselves that same question for our entire careers, but we'd never found the answer to why despicable humans would resort to murdering other humans. Sure, there were usually motives behind most killings—things like jealousy, greed, revenge, hatred—but none of it ever made any sense. There were other ways to resolve those types of problems, but the murderers among us always opted for the easy way out.

Melvin moved out of the grave while Susan helped Amy scoop handfuls of dirt away from Zeke's body. Within another hour, they had removed all of the dirt that surrounded Zeke and his body was resting peacefully atop the damp earth. His last minutes in this world had been anything but peaceful. Blood had gathered on the ground beneath his head and neck, and his face was swollen and bruised. He had been beaten something awful. Due to the lack of mud under his fingernails and the positions of his arms at his sides, I figured he was either already dead or unconscious when he was placed in the grave. At least there was that—he hadn't been buried alive.

"Want me to do the in-person notification?" Susan asked. "I can take Regan with me in case Red gets out of hand."

I glanced at Regan's bandage. "Hasn't she been through enough for her first day?"

Regan immediately shook her head. "I'm not done yet."

I liked her attitude, but didn't feel like smiling, so I only thanked Susan and set out to process the crime scene with Melvin. Amy made her way to the windthrown tree and recovered the shovel. She also searched the area for more evidence, but there were only the partial boot impressions that Melvin had located.

Melvin and I had finished measuring and photographing the scene by the time she returned. I asked if she could help Melvin turn Zeke over so I could photograph the back of Zeke's head. She did so and I took a close-up of his bloody and matted hair. With a gloved hand, I pushed against the back of his skull and shook my head. It was mushy. He had been hit behind the head with a blunt object.

"I think they used the shovel," Amy offered. "When I recovered it, I noticed some hair stuck to the step part of the blade. The shadows were thick in that area, but it looked to match his hair color."

I stood and stepped away from the grave. I surveyed the area, frowning deeply. "We know what Zeke and Paulie were doing out here, but what were the killers doing?"

"That's a good question," Melvin said. "Zeke obviously interrupted something."

Amy nodded her agreement. "Imagine if Brennan Boudreaux hadn't seen their boat or if Zeke's friend hadn't said they had come back here in search of giant catfish. We would've never known to look in this area."

I rubbed my chin. I hadn't shaved this morning and it was obvious. "The killers had no clue Paulie was out there, or they would've tracked him down and killed him, too."

While that might be true, it still didn't tell us why the killers were out there. Knowing we wouldn't solve the mystery by standing around, I walked with Melvin to the boat to retrieve a body bag. Amy stayed behind with Zeke.

Once I had the bag, I asked Melvin if he wanted to tow Zeke's pirogue and boat back to the dock.

"Yeah," he said, "but it might take a while to navigate the shallow water, so don't wait up for me."

I waved and trudged back through the woods to where Amy was waiting patiently. I saw her before she saw me, and I noticed she was staring intently at Zeke, as though she expected him to say something to her. When my boot scraped against a root and made some noise, she looked up and blinked.

"It doesn't make sense that they would bury the kid," she blurted. "No one would ever find his body, so why take the time to dig a six-foot grave and plant him here?"

"That's a good question, but, like all of our questions right now, we don't have answers to them."

"And where did they get the shovel?" Amy whirled around and walked to the evidence package containing the shovel that she'd placed on the ground near our crime scene kit. "Why would they have a shovel in their possession out in the middle of nowhere—unless they were already digging for something?"

I liked where she was going with this theory. "So, you think they were out here digging for something when Zeke happened upon them? You think they killed him because he saw what they were digging up?"

She nodded, but I saw a cloud of doubt wash over her face. "But, other than Zeke's grave, we found no evidence of another dig site, so what the hell?"

"Yeah, if they would've been out here digging, Melvin would've found it."

"Unless they were getting set to dig and Zeke saw the location." She nodded, her confidence growing. "Maybe they had learned of the location of some buried treasure, found the spot, and were about to dig it up when Zeke appeared. They couldn't very well leave the area and let this kid escape with the knowledge of where the treasure was buried. They killed him to keep the secret safe, and they hid the shovel for when they would return later to retrieve the treasure—"

"Or they didn't want to be caught with a murder weapon," I interjected.

Amy paused, then nodded. "Or that."

Her theory was as good as any, but I asked, "If they were digging for treasure, why not retrieve the gold before leaving the area? Surely, they would know that a missing person report would be filed and we would be swarming the area."

"You do have a point." Amy ambled over to the hole and indicated it with a nod of her head. "What if the treasure was in this hole? What if they removed the treasure and replaced it with Zeke's body?"

That was an even better theory, and I said so. "Let's get Zeke out of the hole and see if they left anything behind."

As we began carefully removing Zeke's body from the hole, Amy paused at one point and asked, "What if they were looking for the treasure from the Death Shadow Massacre?"

My head jerked around when she said the words, instinctively searching for anyone who might've overheard her. "I don't even want to think about the Death Shadow Massacre," I said in a low voice. "Too much blood has already been spilt searching for that treasure."

Sensing I didn't want to discuss the issue, Amy only nodded and lifted Zeke's legs while I lifted his upper torso. We were both on our bellies, which was awkward. With a lot of straining and some grunting—and a point when I thought I might spill headfirst into the hole—we finally managed to lift him to the top of the hole and shove him onto high ground.

We scrambled to our feet and I spread the body bag on the ground beside Zeke's body. Once it was unzipped and the flap opened, Amy and I gingerly lifted his body and lowered it into the bag. I had to tuck his arms in so I could zip the bag. After closing it, I sat on the ground and leaned back against a tree, hot and tired. I took a deep breath and closed my eyes for a moment. I slowly exhaled. The air had barely left my lungs when Amy cut loose with a string of obscenities. When she was done cursing, she declared, "There's another body down here!"

CHAPTER 9

"I bet Zeke caught the suspect burying this body and that's why he was murdered," Amy surmised. "It had nothing to do with gold treasures after all."

I was almost afraid to look down the hole. As though having one teenage boy murdered in the woods wasn't bad enough, having two killed would surely throw the entire town into a panic. They might be able to rationalize one killing as an isolated incident that wouldn't affect their children. Maybe the kid was up to no good. He was probably involved in the drug trade or some other illegal activity or he was hanging around with the wrong people. Their kids would never do things like that because they were brought up right.

But if they found out that *two* teens were murdered? Hell, small children would be forced to stay inside, teens wouldn't be allowed in the woods, and parents would arm themselves with every type of weapon imaginable to defend their families against some mysterious and invisible evil stalking the town of Mechant Loup. I grunted to myself. If they ever realized that the majority of murder victims were killed by an acquaintance, they might never go home again.

I rocked forward and crawled to the grave, where I dropped onto my stomach and glanced inside the hole. It was a little after four o'clock and still bright outside, but we were cloaked in the shadows of the surrounding trees and it was dark in the hole. I pushed myself to my knees and was about to head for the crime scene kit to retrieve a flashlight when Amy produced one from her back pocket.

She aimed the beam of light into the hole and we both stared down at the body that had been unearthed by whoever had buried Zeke in this same grave. I cocked my head to the side. The body appeared to be that of a man, based on the discolored long-sleeved shirt—it could have been white or tan at some point—the blue trousers, and the black leather boots, all of which were only partially visible at the bottom of the grave. Most of the body was still covered by mud and I couldn't see the face, but it was obvious that it hadn't been planted here last night.

"It's been down here for years," I said, pointing to a hand protruding from the mud. It was devoid of flesh and tissue. "It's been reduced to a skeleton."

"Shit!" Amy leaned back on her haunches. "What in the hell are we supposed to do with that?"

It wasn't often that I had encountered skeletal remains. I knew we'd need an expert to examine the bones to determine the approximate date of death and to gather identifiable information about the victim. Due to what I could see of the partially unearthed trousers and shirt—they appeared to be the same types of work uniforms my grandpa would wear to work—on the body, my best guess was that it was a male, but I'd need a forensic anthropologist to confirm that for us.

"Okay," I began, stepping back from the hole, "we need to widen the hole so we can get down there and work. If we try to lift the body to the ground level, it'll likely fall apart."

"Even if we widen the hole it'll fall apart when we lift it, so how do we get it out in one piece?"

"We'll have to slide a spinal board under it, tie some ropes to the ends of the spinal board, and lift the spinal board out of the hole." I glanced at the bag that contained Zeke's body. "It's gonna take a while—probably all night—and I want to get Zeke out of here as soon as possible. Out of respect for the kid and his family, I don't want him lying in that mud any longer than he has to."

Amy frowned and nodded. "I'll call the coroner's office."

"Ask them if we can borrow a spinal board while you're at it," I said, and then made my own phone call to Susan. After telling her what we'd discovered, she asked what she could do to help.

"We'll be here all night, so we'll need a large tent, some drop lights, and a generator to run the lights." I paused and scanned our surroundings. "We might also need someone to stand guard while we work. We still don't know who killed Zeke and we don't know the circumstances of this old body. The killer or killers might return to the area, and I don't want them sneaking up on us while we work."

"Okay, I'll get Melvin to bring the equipment, and I'll ask Takecia to meet you out there for security."

"Oh, by the way," I said as an afterthought, "how'd Red McKenzie take the news?"

"Not good at all." She sighed heavily. "Regan and I had to take him to the ground to keep him from hurting himself. We finally got him calmed down. I impressed upon him the importance of being there for Paulie, and that seemed to help."

Amy was still on the phone with the coroner's office when I ended the call with Susan, so I began to carefully widen the grave by digging into the eastern side of the hole. I didn't want to drop any of the fresh dirt on top of the body, so I made sure to take one small scoop of mud at a time and toss it away from the work site. Once Amy had ended her conversation with the coroner's office, she grabbed a shovel and started digging on the opposite end.

Since it was later in the day it was a little cooler, but it was still hot and we were once again dripping sweat within minutes. While the grave had been free of roots, the surrounding ground was not and we had to stop often to chop through them with an axe.

Neither of us spoke until the coroner's investigator arrived on the back of a four-wheeler that was being driven by Takecia Gayle. She smiled when she saw us, but frowned when her eyes found the black bag on the ground that contained the body of Zeke McKenzie.

Takecia was one of Susan's patrol officers who had previously worked the day shift, but had recently been transferred to the night shift thanks to Amy being promoted to detective. Regan would be filling the spot on the day shift previously occupied by Takecia and would be working opposite Melvin, who also worked the night shift. Baylor worked the day shift and would now work opposite Takecia.

Takecia threw her leg off of the four-wheeler and dropped to the ground. Her dark arms glistened with sweat as she reached up and removed her sunglasses. "It's a damn shame what happened to that poor boy," she said in her thick Jamaican accent. "I've answered many calls in town about him being mischievous—just being a boy, you know?—and he was always a nice kid. He called me his girlfriend and said he would marry me when he got old enough."

"Years ago—back before you came to work here—Zeke and Paulie were kidnapped by some bad actors and were left in the attic of an old building," I told Takecia. "Red nearly went crazy and wanted to kill the people responsible. He told me I'd better find the kidnappers before he did, and he meant it. I think it'll be especially true in this case, considering his son was killed. He'll lose his mind. We really need to find out who did this before Red does, because it won't be pretty if he gets to them before we do."

With a renewed sense of urgency, Amy and I continued digging a workable area beside the skeletal remains. Takecia transported the coroner's investigator and Zeke's body back to the end of North Project Road, and returned in fifteen minutes. Melvin was right behind her and he was also on one of the department's four-wheelers. A large tent was secured to the back rack.

Amy and I took a break from digging to help Melvin set up the tent and the generator for the drop lights. While we did that, Takecia—her AR-15 slung across her chest—patrolled the perimeter of our work area. It felt good having her watch our backs. We were able to work without distraction and, within four hours, had dug out a four-by-six-foot area beside the skeletal remains that formed a platform from which we could work to dislodge the body.

I gave Amy a leg up so she could get out of the hole, and she returned the favor by giving me her hand. Every muscle in my body ached. Once I was standing on the ground level, I tossed my shovel aside and twisted to the left and right to work the kinks out of my back. It was completely dark now and mosquitoes were swarming around the drop lights. They had been drilling into us for hours and I was numb to their presence.

"I think Melvin's back," Takecia called from the darkness to our left. He had left an hour ago to get some food for dinner, and we could hear a four-wheeler making its way through the woods. Soon, we caught sight of the ATV's light jostling along the bumpy ride. I walked over to a downed tree nearby and sat wearily on the trunk.

"I'm so hungry I could eat an entire alligator, feet and all," I grumbled.

Amy nodded and plopped down beside me. "You and me—"

"Stop where you are!" Takecia hollered in an authoritative voice. "Stop the four-wheeler and move your hand away from the gun—do it now!"

CHAPTER 10

Instantly upon hearing Takecia's challenge, Amy and I spun off the downed tree—she went to the left and I went to the right—and drew our weapons. Taking cover behind a large cypress tree, I trained my pistol on the light of the four-wheeler and waited for Takecia's lead. I couldn't see Amy, but I knew she'd also sought cover and was covering the ATV.

The four-wheeler had pulled to a stop in response to Takecia's warning, but the engine was still running.

"Lift your hands in the air!" Takecia commanded. "Do it now!"

The sound of her voice indicated to me that she was to my left, and to the right of the driver. The light from the four-wheeler was blinding me, so I couldn't get a bead on the driver. He must've lifted his hands, though, because she issued another command.

"With your left hand, turn off the ATV!"

Without hesitation, the driver killed the engine and the light went dead. In that same moment, Takecia turned on her flashlight and flooded the driver.

I grunted when I saw who it was. "Red, what in the hell are you doing out here?"

He glanced in the direction of my voice and frowned. His eyes were moist and red. It was clear he'd been drinking.

"I...I wanted—" He clamped his mouth shut and I could tell he was trying to contain his emotions.

"I'm moving in," I said to Takecia. I holstered my pistol and stepped out from behind the tree. Once I was within a few feet of Red, I could see that he had a lever-action rifle resting across his legs. "Red, I need to know what you're doing here."

He smacked his lips a few times. Finally, he took a quivering breath and exhaled. "I want to be where he died."

My shoulders drooped. My heart was already broken for him, but I felt even worse.

"He took his last breath right here," Red continued, "and I don't want to be anywhere else."

"Why the rifle?" I asked.

He glanced down at the western-style rifle in his lap. "His killers are still out here somewhere. I brought it just in case I run into them. If I find them before you do, I'm going to kill them, and I don't care who knows it. You won't even have to come looking for me. I'll turn myself in."

Before I could say anything in response, the roaring of at least two other four-wheeler engines sounded through the trees. I stepped closer to Red. "Look, I need you to go home. I understand you want to be where Zeke took his last breath and I respect that, but this is still a crime scene."

Red scowled as he glanced from me to the tent with lights hanging from the poles. "Does it usually take this long to work a crime scene?"

I glanced toward the widened grave. "There's been a development in the case. We've made a discovery that might help answer some questions."

"What kind of discovery?"

The approaching four-wheelers pulled up to the work site and I saw that Melvin was on one and Susan on the other.

"Please, Clint," Red said, "I deserve to know what's going on. It was my son who died."

"Okay," I said, "that's fair enough. When we pulled Zeke out of that hole, we found another body buried down there."

"Another body?" His eyes widened. "But...but who was it?"

"We don't know yet." He started to ask another question, but I raised a hand to stop him. "I can't divulge any more than that. Please, just go back home and take care of Paulie. Once we're done here, we won't have any say over who comes or goes on this property, unless the property owners call and complain. You understand what I'm telling you?"

Red nodded and apologized for interrupting our work. "I'll go home now, but I promise you this: if you don't find them, I will, and I'm going to kill them in the worst way possible."

I didn't say anything as he cranked up his engine and made a wide circle before driving off through the trees. When I turned,

Susan was beside me.

"How're things going out here?"

I told her what we knew so far and explained the plan going forward. She then told me about the fight and arrest she'd made earlier with Regan Steed. As we talked, we joined Melvin and the others and grabbed a hamburger and a Coke from the back rack of Melvin's four-wheeler.

We all sat in a rough circle around the work site and ate our dinner in the glow from the drop lights. The generator hummed softly like soothing background music. I sat there with my friends and my wife, eating home-cooked hamburgers from M & P Grill and making small talk. It might've been easy to forget why we were there, but that big hole wouldn't let me.

I finished eating first and grabbed a pair of latex gloves from my crime scene box. Melvin had strapped a four-foot ladder to the back of his four-wheeler, and I retrieved it. I set it down in the hole and descended to the workable area we'd carved out of the earth.

The drop lights were bright, but there were shadows in the depths of the hole, so I pulled my flashlight from my back pocket and flipped it on. Shining it over the body, I began brushing the soft dirt away from the face. Before long, I'd unearthed the entire head and visually examined it. Something on the right side of the skull caught my attention. I dropped lower in the hole and leaned close.

"What is it?" I heard Susan ask from beside me. "What'd you find?"

"There's a hole in the side of his skull," I said slowly. "It looks like a bullet wound." I leaned back and waved Susan closer. "Check it out."

Susan lowered herself to her knees and squinted as she studied the hole. "Yeah, it sure does look like a bullet hole."

I whipped out my camera and took a picture of the hole, and then continued brushing mud away from the body.

Amy joined Susan and me and started working on unearthing the legs. As I revealed more of the suspect's torso, I found that the shirt was plain and didn't have any logos or any other marks that would help to identify the victim—at least as far as I could see. It was faded and torn in places, and it appeared fragile, so it was possible it could've been marked at one time. I began working on the area just below the waist and frowned when I felt something stiff in the soft mud.

"What's this?"

Susan, who had taken over holding my flashlight, illuminated the area I was currently working on. I raked the dirt away one handful at a time, my curiosity mounting. I sucked in a mouthful of air and whistled out loud when a thick leather belt came into view.

"Holy shit, Sue, he's wearing a gun belt!"

CHAPTER 11

Susan, Amy, and I stared in shock from one to another until a shadow fell across the hole. We looked up to see Melvin standing above us. "He's a cop?"

"I guess so," I said. "He's wearing a leather gun belt. It's old, too." I scraped some of the mud away from the side of the body until I could see more of the belt. There were ammunition loops that extended out of sight under the body. The loops that were visible contained corroded .357 caliber bullets.

I had to reach across the body to dig around the right side, and I did so very carefully. Within minutes, I had unearthed a holster that contained a .357 revolver. It was stainless steel and in surprisingly good condition, by the looks of it.

"He's armed," I said, and then sat back on my heels. I glanced up at Melvin, who had been born and raised in Mechant Loup. "Have you ever heard of a cop going missing in these parts?"

He shook his head. "That would've been big news around here."

"I'll call Mallory and have her check the database of old cases at the sheriff's office," Susan offered. "Maybe he's from the parish."

I nodded, liking the idea. Mallory Tuttle was a detective with the Chateau Parish Sheriff's Office. We worked closely with Mallory and most of the officers at the sheriff's office, but Mallory was more than a fellow officer to my wife—she was one of Susan's closest friends.

As Susan walked to the opposite corner of our enlarged grave, Amy and I continued working to free the skeletal remains. Somewhere off in the distance, I heard a low grumble. I paused, cocked my head to the side. "Is that—?"

"Yep, it's thunder," Amy said. "It's supposed to storm tonight."

"Shit!" I began digging faster with my hands, while still trying not to disturb the body. If it started raining while we were still down here with the body, the hole would start filling up with water within minutes and could destroy any potential evidence that might be on the skeletal remains.

While the tent above would provide shelter from the raindrops, it would do nothing to stop water from spilling into the grave. Nearly all of southeastern Louisiana was in Flood Zone A, but the area in which we found ourselves was especially low.

Amy was grunting at the foot of the body while I continued to clear the ground near the head and shoulders. We needed to dig enough earth away to slide the spinal board under the body, and we were still about twenty minutes away from accomplishing that goal.

"Mallory doesn't remember ever hearing about an officer going missing, but she'll check their records and speak with some of the old timers." Susan dropped beside us and started helping. "She said they do have a couple of outstanding missing person cases from years back, but she doesn't think any of them worked in law enforcement."

I had begun to wonder if this was an ancient burial site and if we were disturbing someone's resting place, but thought better of it. Surely, any respectable lawman would've at least garnered a pine box as a coffin by the sheer virtue of his noble profession. Hell, even outlaws who were hanged in the old days received the benefit of a secure resting spot, so why not this guy? The lack of a coffin at least suggested this was not a sanctioned burial.

No, something sinister had happened at this spot many years ago, and I needed to find out what it was—but to do that, I had to preserve this body as best as I could.

As we worked, the thunder grew louder and lightning began flashing all around us. Soon, I could hear rain pattering against the tent's canopy, and it became stronger with each passing second. Before long, it was coming down in sheets and tiny droplets made their way down to where we were working.

"We need to get the body out of there," Melvin called from above, stating the obvious. "I just checked the forecast—we're about to get a ton of rain dumped on us."

Flash floods were a real problem in Mechant Loup. If we didn't leave in a hurry, we might not be able to make it out of here on the four-wheelers. Unfortunately, the trees were too close together that we would never fit a truck back here.

"Drop the spinal board," I hollered, raising my voice to be heard over the wind, which had begun howling all around us and threatening to rip the canopy from the tent poles.

Much to my dismay, I noticed that water had started flowing into the grave. At first, it was a single tiny trickle in the corner behind me, but then it became more voluminous and several more small waterfalls sprung up.

"How's it looking on your end?" I asked Amy.

"Good enough," she said. "I can get my hands under his legs."

"Can you lift him?"

After a short pause, she cursed. "I think one of his lower leg bones broke loose from his knee."

"Okay, just sit tight." I glanced up and had to squint against the droplets that rained down on me. Melvin appeared in the dim glow from the drop lights and presented the spinal board. He had already fastened a rope to each end of the board, and he held onto the opposite end of one of the ropes while Takecia held onto the opposite end of the other.

Susan and Amy moved back as I took hold of the board. When I placed it down beside the skeletal remains, I realized we were standing in ankle-deep water and the clothes on the body were saturated. "Let's get it under the body," I said.

We all knelt in the water and began scooting the board under the body.

"The water's getting deeper," Amy called over the howling of the wind above us. She was right. Water was gushing down the walls of the hole now and the level had increased an inch within minutes.

Once we'd slid the board under the body, I tugged on one of the ropes. Melvin and Takecia began slowly hoisting the body out of the hole. Susan and I moved to either side of the spinal board and helped guide it up through the hole. The board had almost cleared the ground level when a violent gust of wind blew under the tent and ripped the canopy right off of the poles. There was a loud snap, Takecia cursed, and a torrent of rain slammed down on us.

At that same moment, the end of the board that held the upper portion of the body plunged to the ground. The drop was so sudden that I didn't have time to react and it crashed into the water, throwing the body free.

It was my turn to curse. The water was now about six inches deep and rising fast. The body had crumbled into a loose pile of fabric and bones. I quickly dropped to my knees and tried to find the boots. Susan had scrambled up the ladder and was talking excitedly to

Melvin and Takecia.

Amy placed the spinal board on the flooded ground and moved toward the head of the body. I felt around under the water and my fingers brushed against one of the boots. Working my way upward, I got a grip of the back of the pants with my right hand and slipped my left hand under the lower legs.

Her head only inches from mine, Amy cradled the head and back in her hands. She nodded and said, "I'm ready if you are."

I nodded and we began to lift the body from the water. As soon as it cleared the water, the chunk of fabric I held in my right hand suddenly ripped and the body fell back into the water. I grunted and reached back under the body.

"Clint, I think his arm disconnected from his shoulder," Amy said. "It's just hanging here, connected by the shirt."

I tried to blink away the rain, but it was blinding me. "Let's try to get as much of it as we can on the spinal board," I said. "If we lose any parts of the body, I'll come back for them."

With that said, we managed to scoop the skeletal remains onto the board. The wind was still whipping around up top and I shielded my face as I glanced toward the lights. I couldn't hear any more voices, so I wasn't sure what was happening.

"Susan, is everything okay up there?"

"Yeah, hand me the other rope." Her face hovered just above me. "Takecia took a tent post to the arm. It cut her pretty good, but she's fine."

I handed her the end of the rope that had been flung into the grave when the spinal board fell. Melvin appeared on the opposite side of the hole. As they began reeling in the rope, Amy and I steadied the spinal board to ensure it didn't flip over again. Finally, after a few tense moments, the skeletal remains were above ground. I followed Amy out of the grave and squinted against the blistering rain. Two of the drop lights had shattered when they slammed against the tent poles, so Melvin had shut off the generator. The camcorder was drenched and possibly destroyed.

I checked on Takecia and, thanks to the intermittent lightning strikes, was able to see that her upper arm was bandaged. "You okay?"

"It is nothing," she said, smiling. "Just a splinter."

I smiled back and then watched as Melvin placed a body bag next to the spinal board. The wind kept whipping the plastic edges of the bag around, so Amy and Susan helped him anchor it to the ground. I pitched in and we were finally able to get the spinal board with the skeletal remains into the bag. We were about to zip it up when I remembered the revolver in the holster.

"I need to recover the revolver," I said, hurrying to my crime scene box to retrieve a fresh pair of gloves and a plastic bag. As soon as I got to the police department, I would have to remove the revolver from the plastic and set it out to dry.

Melvin had produced a bright spotlight and was illuminating the holster when I returned. When I pulled on the leather strap that secured the revolver in place, the entire metal snap, which had rusted together, broke loose from the leather. Leaning over the revolver to shield it from the rain, I eased it from the holster and checked the cylinder. There were two live rounds and four spent casings. I could see signs of corrosion around the primers of the non-fired bullets and when I attempted to eject them from the cylinder, they didn't budge.

While Melvin, Susan and Amy zipped the body bag and carefully strapped it to the back rack of Melvin's four-wheeler, I got a zip tie from my box and secured the cylinder in the open position and placed it inside the evidence bag. By the time I was done and the gun was locked in my crime scene box, everyone else was ready to leave the area.

"Clint," Melvin called from the saddle of the four-wheeler.

I walked over and leaned close to hear him over the weather.

"The trail of the suspects has most certainly washed away"—he indicated toward the north—"but they were last heading in that direction. My guess is they veered to the east at some point and hit one of the neighborhoods, where a car was waiting for them."

I nodded, making a mental note to canvass the neighborhoods in Mechant Loup-North as soon as possible.

Takecia—her AR-15 slung across her back—brushed by me and got on the four-wheeler behind Melvin. They headed out immediately. A coroner's investigator was supposed to be waiting for the body at the end of North Project Road. The plan was to have the body transported to the morgue, where a forensic anthropologist would meet with us the next day to examine the body. Zeke's autopsy was also scheduled for the next morning. I didn't relish that one. I hated attending autopsies for women and children.

After securing my crime scene box on the front rack of Susan's four-wheeler, I grabbed my flashlight and approached the grave. I aimed the light into the hole, which was already half filled with muddy water.

"We dug a pond," Amy said. "Maybe we should stock it."

I grunted and gathered up the camcorder and most of our other equipment, knowing we would have to leave some behind. We secured the gear on the back rack of Susan's four-wheeler, wrapped the area of the gravesite in crime scene tape, and then I waved for Amy to jump on the four-wheeler behind Susan.

"What about you?" Amy wanted to know.

"I'll bring up the rear," I said, raising my voice over the roar of the thunder-storm. "I'll let the taillights guide my way."

After hesitating, Amy mounted the four-wheeler and Susan fired it up. They set off into the darkness, just a dark shadow marked by two red lights that jostled through the sheets of rain. I dropped in behind them and plodded through the sloppy mud. It was wet and miserable, but I welcomed the time alone so I could think. I needed to figure out why someone would want to dig up an old grave. Whatever the reason, it had to be bad, because a young boy had been murdered over it.

I tried to keep pace with the ATV, but it was difficult. The mud was mushy and the exposed roots were slick. I stumbled often, but never fell, and kept my eyes trained on the taillights. When lightning would strike, our entire surroundings would brighten up like the daytime and my guiding light would momentarily disappear, only to reappear a second later when darkness enveloped us once again. Each time it happened, those red eyes seemed a little dimmer, and I hoped it wasn't indicative of where my chances of solving this case were heading.

CHAPTER 12

Susan and I woke up to the blaring alarm at seven o'clock the next morning.

"What day is it?" I asked, rubbing the sleep from my eyes.

"You need to stop asking that," Susan mumbled, "or I'm going to have you checked."

It seemed like we'd only been asleep for an hour. After leaving North Project Road, Susan, Amy, and I had met with Melvin and Takecia at the hospital, and the four of us watched as an emergency room doctor stitched up Takecia's arm.

"This is the second officer I've stitched up in twelve hours," the doctor had commented, a frown playing across her face. "What's going on out there?"

Takecia had explained her battle with the tent pole and declared herself the victor. "It was a fierce battle, that you can be assured," she'd said with a gleam in her eyes, "but I won."

Once we'd left the hospital, Susan and I had headed to the police department so I could set the revolver and the camcorder out to dry. Melvin had given Amy a ride to the station, where her car was parked, and they had both gone home to get some sleep. Baylor was covering the night shift for Melvin. Regan was scheduled to be back at the office first thing in the morning, and Susan was going to meet her there to give her a tour of the town.

After I had finished laying out the evidence, I'd met Susan at home and found her in a steaming tub of water. Although we were in the middle of a hot summer, the rain had chilled me to the bone and I'd taken a steaming hot shower while she soaked. We had made idle talk—she'd had to yell most of the time so I could hear her over the shower—while recovering from the cold rain, and had retired to the bedroom feeling refreshed and full of energy. We took full advantage of Grace being away on vacation, and within an hour, that energy was played out.

Now, dragging my legs from the bed and letting them drop to the floor, I was yearning for a day off. Of course, I knew I wouldn't get another day off until I solved this case, so I decided to get to work. Besides, I had to meet with Amy, Dr. Louise Wong, and a forensic anthropologist from La Mort in an hour, so I had to get my ass in gear.

"I had a chance to talk to Gracie yesterday," Susan called from the bathroom. "It sounds like she's having fun with your mom and dad. She doesn't seem to miss us one bit."

I grunted and walked to the sink to brush my teeth. "Speak for yourself. I know she misses me."

Susan had just snapped her bra into place and was reaching for her uniform shirt when she shrieked and cursed out loud.

I spat the toothpaste from my mouth and whirled around. "What is it?"

She had a hand over her mouth and her eyes were wide. She pointed at me. I glanced down at my bare chest.

"What?" I asked, befuddled. "What's wrong?"

"Your back," she said. "It…it looks like someone carved you up with a pitchfork."

I glanced over my shoulder so I could see my back in the mirror. I laughed when I saw the claw marks Susan had dug into my back earlier in the morning. When it had happened, I'd felt the cool burn, but I'd since forgotten about it.

"I guess you'll walk around with my DNA under your fingernails today," I said, still laughing.

"Don't let anyone see that," she said, her face burning red.

I cocked my head to the side. "And who in the hell's gonna see my bare back at work? I don't normally walk around sans shirt when I'm hunting down bad guys."

"I don't know." She still seemed to be in shock. "Just don't let it happen."

As I continued brushing my teeth, she walked over and rubbed her fingers gently across my back, retracing the claw marks. I didn't know if she was really horrified or simply proud of her handiwork, but I interrupted her by pulling on my shirt.

"I've got to go," I said, kissing her before walking to my closet to finish getting dressed. "I don't want to be late for the autopsy—or bone examination."

"No breakfast?"

"I'll grab something on the way out," I called over my shoulder. I snapped my pistol in place and rushed downstairs, where Achilles and Coco were waiting for me. My heart sank when I saw the look in Achilles' eyes. He wanted to come with me. I dropped to my knees so I could look him in the eyes. "I'm sorry, Big Man, but I've got work to do. I'd bring you along, but you don't want to see what's about to happen—especially to little Zeke McKenzie."

He cocked his head to the side, as though trying to understand the words that were spilling from my mouth.

"Don't make like you don't understand me," I scolded. "Your English is better than mine."

CHAPTER 13

Amy was waiting for me in the parking lot at the coroner's office when I arrived. My cell phone started ringing before I could get out of my Tahoe. I didn't recognize the number, but answered anyway.

"This is Clint," I said and waited for a response.

"Did you find the man who killed my son?"

I sighed heavily when I recognized Red McKenzie's voice. "Hey, Red, I'm sorry, but we don't have anything yet. I'm just arriving at the coroner's office. Dr. Louise Wong will perform the autopsy on Zeke and we'll know exactly what happened to him within a few hours. They're also set to examine the body that was buried in the same grave as Zeke. Please don't repeat this, but it appears it's been there for many years—maybe decades. If we can somehow identify that body, it might lend some insight into what happened out there Monday night."

There was a long pause on the other end. Finally, Red spoke again. "Please let me know as soon as you find out anything. I want to know what's going on. I want you to find who did this."

"Yes, sir," I said, frowning. "I'm real sorry, Red."

"Why are you sorry?" he retorted. "Did you kill my boy?"

"No, sir."

"Then don't be sorry—just catch that son of a bitch!"

Before I could respond, the call ended. I sat there for a moment. Despite his wishes, I did feel sorry for the man. He probably felt as though it was his sole responsibility to protect his sons, and one of the boys had been taken on his watch, while he lay asleep at home. In addition to the tremendous amount of sorrow that had overcome him and the intense rage that was burning inside of him, he was probably also experiencing some level of guilt.

Amy raised her hands as though wanting to know if I was ready to go inside. She couldn't see me through my tinted windows, but she was staring right at me. I opened the door and dropped to the ground.

"Red McKenzie just called me," I explained.

"Oh, jeez, I feel bad for that poor man."

I nodded and grabbed my camera before following Amy into the morgue. Dr. Wong and her assistant were garbed-out and they were prepping Zeke's body for autopsy. She glanced up when we walked in.

"Hey, gang, nice to see you two again." She frowned through her clear face shield. "Why is it that we keep meeting like this? Why can't we run into each other in the grocery store or the park or some other place?"

"We shop at different stores?" I offered. "And I don't go to the park?"

"That makes sense." She indicated Zeke's body. "What's the story with this young man?"

I told her what we knew so far. She listened intently until I was done.

"So," she said, "the skeletal remains in the other cooler were found under this body in the same grave?"

I nodded.

"Wow—two bodies found in the same grave, but put there at vastly different periods in time." Her brow was furrowed. "I don't know that I've ever heard of such a thing being done, except through a funeral home."

I tried to think back through all of the cases I'd worked over the years, and—like Dr. Wong—I couldn't remember anything like this ever happening before. As I considered her words and watched her begin Zeke's autopsy, I picked up where I'd left off last night in trying to figure out this case.

It was definitely an odd one, and I had no clue where the evidence would take us—provided we would develop more evidence along the way. A sense of panic threatened to rear its ugly head within my chest, as I considered the possibility of the trail going cold right here in the morgue. There were no cameras in the woods and there had been no potential witnesses. Sure, we would canvass the neighborhoods around North Project Road, but the chances were slim that anyone would know anything.

Amy photographed the autopsy and I took notes while Dr. Wong worked on Zeke. A thorough pathologist, she didn't leave a stone unturned when trying to determine a cause of death or trying to recover evidence from his body, and it was four hours before she was done.

She had already told us the manner of death would be ruled a homicide and the cause of death was blunt force trauma, consistent with being hit in the back of the head with a shovel. She'd also determined that he had been beaten while he was on the ground.

"It appears he was stomped in the face while he was on the ground," she had said, pointing out the injuries for Amy to photograph. "Whoever did this to him wanted to make sure he wouldn't regain consciousness and dig his way out of that grave."

While her assistant moved Zeke's body back to one of the coolers and cleaned off the stainless steel autopsy table, Dr. Wong removed her personal protective equipment and washed off in preparation for the examination of the skeletal remains.

"Mary Roach—she's a renowned forensic anthropologist—will be here after lunch and she'll do a preliminary, but then she'll transport the remains to her lab for a more thorough examination," Dr. Wong explained. "I'll do an autopsy before she takes the body away, in the hopes that we can get some immediate answers."

Amy and I stood around waiting while the assistant took the skeletal remains from the cooler and brought them to be x-rayed. When he was done, he and Dr. Wong transferred the body onto the autopsy table and then she brought the film into the room. Once she'd snapped the first film onto the viewer, she grunted.

"Well," she said, "this looks like a bag of puzzle pieces."

I shifted my feet. "Yeah, we had a bit of an accident while trying to get him out of the ground."

"Understandable." She glanced in our direction. "That was one hell of a storm that blew through here last night. Most people would've left the body there and gone back for it later."

She put the next film on the viewer and immediately pointed to four bright spots on the left side of the jaw. "He got his jaw broken at some point," she explained. "They had to insert pins for support."

"That can help with the identification, right?" I asked, feeling hopeful.

"Absolutely, but we need a name first," she explained. "Without a name, we wouldn't even know where to begin looking. There's no database we can access that lists everyone who had pins inserted in their jaws—but wouldn't that be cool?"

I nodded, thinking it was not impossible to think it could happen in the future. After all, merely forty years ago no one would've thought we'd have an international database of DNA profiles.

Dr. Wong suddenly leaned close to study a spot on the X-ray. She squinted. It appeared that something had caught her attention. Without saying a word, she pulled on some gloves and hurried to the table. Her assistant had cleaned off the bones that were protruding from the clothes, and she titled the skull away from her.

When she moved the skull, I heard something rattle inside the skull. Amy and I glanced at each other and joined Dr. Wong.

"What'd you find?" I asked.

"It appears there's a bullet hole in the right side of the parietal bone, and something is rattling around inside his skull." She grabbed a set of long alligator forceps and carefully guided it through an opening in the skull. When she withdrew the forceps from the hole, it held a small object. It appeared to be a lead projectile and the striations from the bore of the weapon that fired it were still present at the base of the bullet. "Eureka! This man was shot in the head, and this is the bullet that killed him."

CHAPTER 14

I indicated the empty holster and said to Dr. Wong, "There was a loaded revolver in that holster, and four bullets had been fired."

She nodded, considering what it might mean while she secured the bullet in a small evidence collection container. She then handed it to her assistant, so he could write the recovery date and time on the attached label.

"What do you think happened?" she asked. "One bullet in the head, four fired rounds, and the gun ends up in his holster? Pretty strange."

"Yeah, it is strange." I shrugged. "I guess it's possible someone put the revolver back in the holster when they buried him, but I've got no clue what happened before he was buried. It's anyone's guess, really."

Dr. Wong leaned close to the skull and examined the hole. "The wound is nice and circular, so it wasn't a contact wound. As you already know, this suggests it wasn't self-inflicted."

I glanced where she pointed and nodded my agreement when I saw the clean hole. I also marveled at the condition of the skull. It looked a lot different than it had last night, when mud was clumped into the eye sockets and smeared across the entire surface. Even the clothes looked different, now that the mud had been rinsed off of it. The shirt appeared to be a khaki shirt, although it had seen much better days, and the pants were dark-colored, maybe navy blue at one time.

We watched intently as the assistant carefully removed the clothes. The fabric had dried out in the ground over the years and the fabric was brittle. When he had cut off the pants and spread them out on an examination table, I noticed that the right seat of the pants was hanging loose. I tapped my chest.

"That was me," I explained. "I was trying to slide him onto a spinal board and the pants ripped."

"Is there anything in the pocket?" Amy asked.

The assistant checked the dangling pocket, shook his head. He checked the other back pocket, and it was also empty. He then reached his slender hand into the front pockets. I held my breath as he withdrew his hand. It was empty.

I glanced at Amy as the assistant checked the last pocket. She shrugged and, like me, I knew she wasn't expecting much. We were right.

"Thirty-seven cents." The assistant rinsed off the coins and then held them up in his palm. "One quarter, one dime, and two pennies. That's it—nothing else."

"He must've definitely been a cop," Amy mumbled. "He was broke when he died, just like I'll be."

I nodded my agreement as I studied the coins in the palm of the assistant's hand. They had been pretty well preserved, and the quarter appeared shiny new. I was about to move away from the examination table when a thought occurred to me. "Hey, how old are those coins?"

The assistant pulled them close and examined them one at a time, water still dripping from his hands. "The quarter is from thirty-three years ago, one of the pennies is from thirty-eight years ago, the other penny is from forty-two years ago, and the dime is from thirty-five years ago."

"So, the most recent coin was from thirty-three years ago," I mused allowed. "If these coins were dated the years they were produced, then we know he could've been in the ground for up to thirty-three years, but not longer."

"What about the shirt pockets?" Amy asked the assistant. "Anything in them?"

He checked the shirt pockets, but shook his head.

Next, he laid the gun belt and holster out on a table, where Amy and I could visually examine it. I was hoping for a name or some other type of identifier stamped into the back of the weathered leather, but we had no such luck. Every loop was filled.

"What kind of gun was it?" Dr. Wong asked as she busied herself working on the skeletal remains.

"A Ruger GP-100, which first came into production about thirty-four years ago," I explained, still checking the leather. "The timeframe is consistent with the coins. I'll be able to narrow it down further by checking the serial number on the gun."

"You can do that?" she asked.

"Yep." I checked the bullets that were shoved into the loops of the gun belt. They were heavily corroded, but I was able to copy the information on the headstamp, which confirmed they were all .357 caliber cartridges.

"There's nothing here, Clint," Amy said with a sigh after we'd gone over the items carefully, photographing each as we inspected them.

I turned away from the table and approached Dr. Wong. She was studying the skeletal remains closely. Some of the bones had broken loose from the torso during the spill, and she was now piecing the body back together like a full-size puzzle.

I shifted my feet, feeling restless. "Hey, Doc, how long do you think this'll take?"

"Oh, I'll be here a while." She paused and looked at me through the face shield. "We've got to measure every bone, inspect them for evidence of old fractures or medical procedures, search for signs of injury, and on and on. It could easily take a few days to complete a thorough examination."

"What can your examination possibly reveal?"

"We can determine the individual's gender and approximate age, and Mary can reconstruct the face for a possible identification."

As I figured, nothing they discovered would be of immediate assistance in solving the case, and I mentioned as much.

"You're right," Dr. Wong acknowledged. "Most of what we find will help to verify his identification and to tell a story about what happened to him, but your investigation will have to uncover some possible names for comparison purposes. If we have to wait for Mary to reconstruct his face so we can send a photo out to the media for identification, I'm afraid we'll be waiting a long time."

That was all I needed to hear. After collecting the gun belt and the projectile for evidence—I left the clothes behind to be examined by Dr. Mary Roach—I asked Dr. Wong to call if she needed anything, and then I waved for Amy to follow me.

"Where're we going?" Amy asked once we were outside.

I frowned when I saw the sheets of rain pouring down all around us. I wanted to go back to the burial site, but it would be impossible to inspect the hole in this rain. Had it not been raining, I could've pumped out the hole and started inspecting it further, but at this rate, the hole would be filling faster than any pump could drain it.

"We need to divide and conquer," I finally said to Amy. "One of us needs to bring the evidence to the crime lab and the other needs to canvass the neighborhoods surrounding North Project Road. I think it'll be a waste of time, but it needs to be done just in case someone saw or heard something that might help to break this case wide open—because right now, we've got nothing. We need to get with the local papers and research articles from—say—twenty to thirty-three years ago to find out if a lawman ever went missing. We also need to go to the assessor's office and find out the next of kin for that plat of land. They might've heard rumors about something taking place thirty-plus years ago on their land."

"I'll take the crime lab and the assessor's office," she said without hesitation.

I nodded and we jogged to our vehicles and headed back to the police department. Once we'd arrived, we met Susan and Regan in the break room. I grabbed a handful of paper towels to wipe the rain from my face and hair. I then started making a sandwich.

"Regan rolls into town and suddenly the skies open up," Amy said playfully from the other side of the room. "That girl's always been trouble. I can tell y'all some stories."

Regan shot an evil look in Amy's direction. "Keep it up and I'll tell them about that one night in college."

Amy shook out her blonde hair and water dripped down her shoulders. She smiled. "I don't regret anything I've ever done, but—"

"You do regret not doing a few things," Regan said, finishing Amy's sentence. The two women laughed. Amy patted her hair dry with a towel from the kitchen drawer and then began making herself a sandwich.

"Anything come out of the autopsy?" Susan asked, twisting around in her chair to see me.

As I put the finishing touches on my triple-decker sandwich, I told her what we'd learned. "Basically, we've got a guy—possibly a cop—who was shot in the head and buried. Thanks to some coins in his pocket, we think he's been dead for up to thirty-three years. His gun was still in his holster and might provide a more accurate timeframe. There was also a projectile rolling around in his head that might help identify the murder weapon—if we ever find one."

I took my plate and sat across from Susan and Regan while I continued. "On Monday night, decades after he was planted, someone decides to dig him up—for Lord knows why—but a young boy interrupts that process and ends up buried on top of the man.

That about sums it up and it makes no sense whatsoever."

"Could it have been a suicide?" Susan wanted to know. "What if his family buried his body to hide the fact that he committed suicide? Suicide is taboo in some circles. Hell, they might've done it for the insurance money. After so many years of being missing, can't the missing person be declared dead and the insurance company forced to pay up? Wait a minute"—her face scrunched up—"I was barely born thirty-three years ago. Did they even have life insurance back then?"

I was chewing on a mouthful of food and almost choked from laughing. When I swallowed, I said, "It wasn't a contact wound and, while it's possible he held the gun away from his head and shot himself, I'm thinking it was a homicide. If you're going to kill yourself, you want to make sure you do it right. Holding the gun away from his head would've increased the chances of a failed attempt."

Regan tucked a lock of long, black hair behind her ear and asked, "What if the bullet in his head was fired from the gun in his holster?"

I stopped chewing and stared at her. She had porcelain skin, which would probably burn red in the Louisiana sun.

"I wouldn't like that one bit," I finally said.

"Why not?" she asked. "Wouldn't it be good to have the murder weapon?"

"I'd rather find the murder weapon in the hands of the killer, rather than in the holster of the victim." I sighed. "If the murder weapon and the victim are found in the same hole, and if we can't get DNA from the weapon, we're dead in the water—literally."

CHAPTER 15

After our late lunch, Amy headed for the crime lab with the evidence and the scientific analysis request sheet in her hand. We were asking for the revolver to be scrubbed for DNA and then tested against the projectile to hopefully exclude it from being the murder weapon. If our victim had been killed with his own weapon, then I'd have to seriously consider the fact that he might have taken his own life. While difficult to pull off, crazier things had happened.

As for me, I'd asked Lindsey to run the Ruger revolver through the NCIC database to see if it had ever been reported stolen, but there was no record on file. Next, I sent out a request to the ATF for a weapon's trace, and then I began researching the serial number to determine the production date.

I started on Ruger's website and found a chart that displayed a list of serial numbers in a column to the left, with the corresponding year of production in a column to the right. I checked my notes for the weapon's serial number and slid my finger down the sheet to find where it fit. I smiled.

"What're you smiling about?" Susan asked from my doorway. "Did you break the case?"

"Oh, hey there, Mountain Lion," I said, leaning back in my chair and gingerly reaching for my shoulder where she had clawed me earlier in the morning during sex. "I didn't see you standing there."

Her tanned face suddenly turned red and she shot a quick glance up and down the hall. "Don't say that! Someone will hear you."

"I was able to pinpoint the outer edge of the burial time period," I said, ignoring her admonition. "The weapon in our victim's holster was produced thirty years ago, so he couldn't have purchased it before then. This means he was buried within the last thirty years—no earlier."

"And this helps us how?"

"I don't know yet." I jumped to my feet and pulled on my raincoat. I then grabbed my notebook. "I'm off to canvass Mechant Loup-North. Maybe I'll get lucky."

"Want some company?" she offered. "Regan's riding around with Baylor and I've got some time."

I welcomed the help and we headed out together. We began at the Mechant Loup bridge, on the western side of the highway, and worked our way north through each neighborhood. She took one side of the street and I took the other. There were short breaks in the rain, but, for the most part, we were rained on most of the time. It was hard to keep the pages in our notebooks dry, but it didn't really matter, because we learned nothing of substance.

Once we'd knocked on every door on every street on the western side of the highway, we switched to the eastern side and began canvassing those neighborhoods. When we reached the end of North Boulevard, I leaned in close to Susan, allowing my hood to overlap hers so she could hear me over the driving rain.

"Remember that house?" I pointed to a mansion at the end of the street. We had worked a heinous murder case in front of that house some time back, and it had made a lasting impression on most of us.

She nodded. "How could I ever forget?"

We walked up the long driveway together and rang the doorbell, but no one answered. Turning, we continued working our way to the north, and ended up completing the canvass an hour later.

Before heading back to the office, I drove to the end of North Project Road, crossed the wooden bridge, and parked on the headland. I shut off my engine.

"What're you thinking?" Susan asked, looking from me to the rain pounding the windshield.

"I want to check out the gravesite."

"Let's do it."

We were already wearing our rubber boots, so we dumped out of my Tahoe and lowered our heads against the driving rain. We started the long hike through the woods. Once we hit the trees, the umbrella of branches and leaves above us offered some reprieve from the relentless downpour, but it did nothing to help the saturated ground. The water was at least eight inches deep in most areas, but reached the top edges of our boots in some places.

It was only five o'clock in the afternoon, but the dark clouds and trees made it appear closer to nine, so we were forced to pull out our flashlights.

"If this rain doesn't stop," Susan hollered over the thunder that rumbled overhead, "we'll never be able to retrieve the tent."

I nodded and paused to wipe water out of my eyes and check our surroundings. I didn't recognize a single landmark and the ground had been reduced to a shallow pond. Susan nudged my arm and pointed to our right, where her flashlight illuminated an alligator that was lounging on a log. It looked to be a little more than seven feet long.

"I bet they're everywhere" she said, drawing her pistol. "I'm not getting eaten by an alligator today. I'm just not in the mood."

I had personally watched a man lose his arm and nearly his life to an alligator, so I wasn't about to object to her level of apprehension. My eyes finally fixed on a tree to our left. I recognized it and headed in that direction. It was a lucky find. Once we reached it, I saw the yellow police tape flapping in the wind about a hundred yards away.

"We're almost there." I pointed in that direction, where a giant oak tree stood guard over the crime scene. "There's the gravesite."

Encouraged by the sighting, Susan pushed by me and high-stepped it to the area. Once we'd reached the crime scene tape, she scanned our surroundings until she found a downed tree that was sticking out of the water. Without hesitation, she grabbed onto a branch and pulled herself out of the water. She didn't holster her pistol.

"You okay, Love?" I asked, amused.

"I swear, if an alligator comes by me, I'm blasting his ass straight to hell."

I laughed and ducked under the crime scene tape. I could see the mound of dirt we'd created by digging out the grave. It was now a mess of wet mud and it helped to orient me to the large hole that was hidden somewhere under the surface of the water. The tent poles would have helped to pinpoint the grave, but most of them had been snapped and were now tangled in the trees about ten feet to the south. The canopy had been shredded into several pieces, one of which was still attached to some of the broken tent poles.

As I splashed through the water, I caught movement several feet away from me. I glanced in that direction and saw a large cottonmouth swimming on the surface of the water. It was heading in Susan's direction, so I pointed it out to her.

Susan kept her pistol lowered. "As long as it isn't a frog. If I see a frog, you'd better take cover, because I can't guarantee where my bullets will go."

I laughed and watched the snake, but it changed directions and headed toward the southwest, where the lake was hidden from view by the trees. I strolled through the water, encircling the gravesite, searching—for what, I wasn't sure. I was hoping the water might have forced something up from the ground. I had also hoped the killer or killers had returned to the scene and we'd catch them here, but that apparently hadn't happened.

The rain continued to find its way through the trees and pepper the earth. After about ten minutes, Susan asked, "What're we looking for?"

She had gotten down from the tree and was warily approaching my location.

"I don't know." A stream of water had found an opening under my collar and leaked all the way down my back. I shivered. Was it only in Louisiana that I could suffer a heat stroke one day and be left shivering the next day? I finally decided it was no use. "Let's get out of here."

Neither of us spoke on the walk back to my Tahoe. Once we were inside the dry vehicle, I checked my cell phone. I had seven missed calls. One from Amy, one from Lindsey, and five from Red McKenzie.

I called Lindsey first. "What's up?"

"Where are you, Clint? Red McKenzie called a dozen times looking for you. He's really mad."

"I know. He called my cell five times. Is that all?"

"No, two reporters called back to say they can't find a record of a missing cop—who's missing, by the way?"

"It's about that body we found. Anything else?"

"Yeah, you received a fax from the ATF."

"It's the firearms trace report. Can you read what it says?"

"It says the firearm you made the request on was purchased at a dealer who's no longer in business." There was a pause, and I imagined she was scanning the report, but I'd heard enough.

"So, basically, there's no record of the purchase."

"That's what it seems."

"Okay, thanks."

"Call Red McKenzie," she said hurriedly as I was ending the call. "He won't stop calling."

Before calling Red, I called Amy. "Please tell me you were calling with good news."

"The good news is we got a match on the bullet."

I groaned inwardly. "And the bad news is he was shot with his own gun, wasn't he?"

"You win."

"Damn it."

Susan arched an eyebrow. I told her what Amy had just told me and then turned back to the call.

"Anything else?" I asked.

"They swabbed it for DNA before test-firing it," she said. "Considering it's been secured in the holster for years, they think the chances are high that they'll be able to recover DNA evidence."

At least there was that. I thanked her and fired up my Tahoe. I called Red as I drove up North Project Road, and he answered the phone cursing.

Once there was a break in the onslaught of profanity, I assured him we were doing everything we could to find Zeke's killer. "I'll be perfectly honest with you Red, this case will probably take some time—"

"I don't want to hear that shit!" he bellowed. "I want you to find the man who killed my son!"

Based on what I already knew of the case, I was afraid to make any promises, so I simply said, "I'll do everything I can."

"Damn it, Clint," Red hollered in a threatening manner, "you'd better get off your ass and solve this case or I'm going to start taking the law into my own hands."

I could've said a lot of things in response. I could've told him I wanted his son's murder solved almost as much as he did, or that I was doing my best to catch his son's killer, or that I'd been where he was and I understood. However, none of those things would've mattered to the poor man, and I certainly was not offended by his words. He had every right to feel the way he felt.

"Yes, sir, I understand," was all I said.

There was a long pause on the other end. Finally, he took a deep breath and exhaled forcefully. When he spoke again, his voice was as soft as he could muster. "Do you have any leads? Anything at all?"

"We've learned that the body in the grave has been there for at least thirty years," I explained. "It was a male subject and he died by a single gunshot wound to the head. We also think he might've been a cop or some kind of security guard, considering his clothes appeared to be some type of uniform and he wore a gun belt with a loaded gun in the holster."

"But...what does this have to do with Zeke? What was he doing near this grave?"

"I think he stumbled onto something and he was killed because of what he saw." Susan and I had reached the police department and I parked under the building, where the harsh pounding on the roof of my Tahoe suddenly ceased and things grew quieter inside. "I really believe the key to solving this case is to identify the man in the grave. We've got forensic anthropologists working—"

"Forensic what?"

"They're doctors who specialize in identifying human remains. We've got a good one working the case."

"How long will it take to identify the man?"

I sighed. "It might take a while, but I'm not waiting on them to identify him. We've got someone researching the property records in hopes of identifying the land owners. That might open some doors. I find it hard to believe a body would've been buried on the land without someone in the family knowing something about it."

"How long will that take?"

I glanced around the parking area under the police department and noticed Amy's Dodge Charger parked in the corner. "I'm about to meet with the detective who was doing that research and I should have an answer for you by the morning."

When he didn't say anything for a while, I said, "But I don't think I'll be sharing that information with you."

"And why is that?" he demanded to know.

"I don't want you tracking them down and trying to beat the information out of them."

CHAPTER 16

"Mark and Tami Boudreaux," Amy said when I asked her if she'd found out who owned the property behind North Project Road. "They used to live in a house about two hundred yards north of the gravesite. The house sits on an acre of cleared land with a long driveway that stretches to the highway. The driveway is private and it's located about a mile north of North Project Road."

"Do you have a map of the area?" I asked.

It was a little after six o'clock in the evening and we were sitting in Susan's office. Susan was behind her desk, I was in a chair across from her, and Amy sat beside me. When I asked about the map, Amy stood and walked around to Susan's side of the desk. I joined them.

"I'm not sure how long ago this satellite image was captured," she said, pointing to a cleared area amidst a large tract of woodlands, "but you can see the clearing right here. Their property lies beyond the end of North Project Road and it encompasses the private lake or pond where Zeke and Paulie were searching for giant catfish."

"How old are they—this Mark and Tami Boudreaux?"

"Mark died a few years ago, when he was ninety-three," Amy explained. "His wife is in a nursing home. She's eighty-four."

I leaned my back against the wall behind Susan's desk. "Do they have any children?"

"Just one son—Albert, fifty-six—but he doesn't live around here." Amy pulled her notebook from the waistband of her jeans and thumbed through it. "I ran his name and found an address for him in a small county in Colorado. I've got his number, but I figured I'd talk to you before calling him."

I folded my arms across my chest and pondered this new

information. "How long has the son lived in this county?"

"It appears he left home thirty-eight years ago and he's moved around a lot as a young man, but he's been in Sage County for about twenty years now." Amy shrugged. "Give or take a year."

Susan leaned back in her swivel chair. "I guess he wasn't around when the body was buried."

"Unless he was down here visiting at the time," Amy suggested. "What if he came down here to visit and got in trouble with the law? What if he killed a deputy or a police officer, buried said officer or deputy, and then went back out West, never to be heard from again?"

"But that kind of thing wouldn't just die out," I said. "When a cop is killed, that's big news—and rightly so. If criminals are so lawless that they'd kill a cop, there's nothing they wouldn't do. Those kinds of cases definitely make local news—sometimes get the attention of the national news—but interest usually dies out after the funeral, picks up again during the suspect's trial, and then dies out after the conviction."

Susan glanced up at me as though to say, "What's your point?"

"Now, imagine that we have a missing cop, who disappears into thin air, never to be heard from again," I suggested. "How intriguing do you think that would be? It would be a true-to-life mystery. It would excite the curiosity of every news organization in the nation. The story would never die, because the disappearance was never solved—there was never any closure. A trial, a funeral—those things provide levels of closure. A missing cop case would've been huge. Hell, it would've probably even been featured on Unsolved Mysteries, which was running back then."

"What if it was featured on Unsolved Mysteries?" Susan asked.

I thought back to when I used to watch Unsolved Mysteries as a young boy. It was my favorite show on television at the time. Robert Stack's legendary and mysterious voice set the tone for the show, and I never watched any of the episodes after he was gone. I'd heard that there were a few episodes before he started hosting the show, but I never watched any of those either.

I couldn't remember seeing an episode that involved a missing cop, but then again, I couldn't remember the details of every case. Besides, I grew up around La Mort and I hadn't even heard of Mechant Loup back then, so the story might not have resonated with me, or it could've aired after I'd quit watching.

I glanced over at Amy. "Did you run a background check on Mark and Tami Boudreaux?"

"Yeah, they've been clean their entire lives—as far as I can tell."

The corner of her mouth curled into a grin. "I don't know if they gave out tickets to people on horse buggies or if they kept records before the ink pen was invented, but their modern-day driving record seems to be clean."

"What about the local papers?" Susan asked. "Anything there?"

I shook my head. "I put in calls to them earlier in the day, but they left messages with Lindsey saying they had nothing."

"This case is scary," Amy said.

"How's that?" I asked.

"We've got absolutely nothing to go on—not one shred of evidence that might identify the killer. What if we never solve it?" She tucked a lock of blonde hair behind her ear. "What if we never find the person who killed the old cop or Zeke? We're up against a wall, with nowhere to go."

"Every interview, every document, every piece of evidence should lead somewhere else." I pointed to the map on the computer screen. "What you found is important. It leads us to Tami Boudreaux and her son, Albert."

"What if the husband planted that body in the woods?" Amy challenged. "He's dead now, so he won't be talking."

"He might've planted that body years ago, but he certainly didn't dig it up or kill Zeke, unless he came out of the grave himself to do it. Our suspect is out there somewhere and we're gonna find him— one way or another." I stood straight and stretched. "I'm heading home, Sue. Amy, let's meet here first thing in the morning. We'll call Albert Boudreaux and see what he knows, and then we'll pay a visit to the nursing home."

So saying, I walked out and drove home. When Susan arrived an hour later, I was sitting on the sofa watching reruns of Unsolved Mysteries and doing research on my laptop. Achilles was stretched out on my left side and Coco on the right, each of them with their snout shoved up close to me.

"And where am I supposed to sit?" Susan wanted to know as she unzipped her uniform shirt.

I leaned forward, rested the laptop on the coffee table, and then slapped my thighs. Without hesitating, she covered the distance between us and threw herself in my lap. The weight of her body stretching out over mine felt good, and I wrapped my arms around her. Achilles had scooted closer and was now resting his head across Susan's legs. Not to be outdone, Coco had also moved closer and nestled against Achilles.

I had sped through six episodes of Unsolved Mysteries and

searched the internet for missing cops. While there had been quite a few reports of missing officers over the years, most of them had already been located—some dead, some not—and none of the cases was remotely close to what was happening here.

"Any luck?" Susan asked, indicating my laptop on the coffee table.

"Nothing so far."

We had the fixings for leftover tacos and burritos, and I was about to suggest a quick bite before going upstairs for a conversation, when Susan's cell phone made that strange sound it made when someone was doing a FaceTime call. I had never learned how to do it, and I didn't care to learn, but I was very excited to see Grace's face pop up on the screen. Her cheeks were red like her hair and it appeared a few new freckles had formed on her forehead. She looked like she'd grown an inch since last weekend.

"Hey, Gracie," I said, as Susan and I rested our heads against each other to see the screen on her phone. "How are you?"

"Daddy!" she squealed.

I reached up and gave Susan's right hip a squeeze. "I told you she misses me."

CHAPTER 17

I arrived at the police department at seven-thirty the next morning. The rain had stopped during the night. The meteorologist from New Orleans had come on this morning to warn that the smothering heat would be returning by this afternoon. I was happy to see the rain stop, but I wasn't sure how I felt about the "swamp booty" returning.

Amy showed up ten minutes after I did and met me in my office. I had already spoken with Red McKenzie—he had called before I even left my house—and I told Amy about the call. All in all, he was a lot calmer than the day before, but he was still threatening to take matters into his own hands if we didn't solve the case soon.

When Amy was seated across from me, I grabbed a notebook, set up my recorder, and pressed the speaker button on my desk phone. I glanced up at her. "Ready?"

She gave a nod and I dialed the number for Albert Boudreaux.

Boudreaux was a common family name in Louisiana and there might be a dozen Alberts running around Chateau Parish, but I was pretty positive there could be only one Albert Boudreaux in Sage County, Colorado.

"Hey, Mom, is that you?" asked a man with a flat voice. I was proud to hear he hadn't lost his Cajun accent.

"No, sir, this is Clint Wolf," I said, leaning close to the phone. "I work for the Mechant Loup Police Department. Is this Albert?"

"Um, yeah." There was a hint of hesitation in the man's voice. "Is…is this about my mom?"

"Oh, no, this is about a case I'm working," I said quickly.

I heard a deep sigh on the other end. It sounded like he was on speaker phone, too, and I could hear some movements in the background.

"The only calls I get with that area code are from my mom," he explained. "You scared me half to death."

"I'm sorry about that." After a brief pause, I made small talk with him, asking him mostly about life in Colorado versus life in Louisiana, and then I asked how often he came to visit.

"I come down at least once a year, around Christmas, to see my mom, and I try to make a trip during the summer, although I'm not always able to get away from work. I made five trips to Louisiana three years ago, when my dad died." He took a breath and exhaled. "I went down there when he was sick and stayed a week. I went back for the funeral a month later, but had to go back to look in on my mom the following week. It was obvious she wouldn't be able to care for herself, so I had to put her in an assisted living home. There are people to look after her, but she's got her own apartment and has complete freedom to come and go as she pleases. I visited her for Christmas and she seems to be enjoying it. I promised to visit her every Christmas, so we'll be heading there in December."

"Are you married?" I asked. "Do you have any kids?"

"I'm married," he said easily enough, but he seemed to be growing suspicious. "We've got three kids—a boy and two girls. Why do you ask?"

"About the kids? Oh, I was just making small talk. I've got one of my own—a fiery little redhead." I decided to shift gears. "When was the last time you came to Louisiana? More specifically, to the family home in Mechant Loup?"

"About seven months ago, for Christmas. Why?"

"Look, what I'm about to tell you is part of an active criminal investigation and I need you to keep this information to yourself." I paused to give him time to process what I'd just said. "Can I count on you to keep this quiet?"

"A criminal investigation?"

"Can I count on you to keep this quiet?"

"Sure, but I don't know what you're talking about."

I shifted in my chair and told him the whole story, beginning with the search for Zeke and Paulie and ending with two dead bodies we found on his family's property. He seemed genuinely shocked.

"I...I don't know what to say. Are you accusing me of something? Do you think I did this?"

"To be quite candid, I don't know who did this and it's possible it could've been you."

"Oh, no!" he said with complete confidence. "I had nothing to do with a dead body on any property!"

"Can anyone there verify your whereabouts for the past week or so?" I asked.

"Yep! My wife, my kids, and my job can all verify that I was right here in Colorado almost every day since Christmas. The only time we left the state was in February to do some snow skiing in Sundance."

"Sundance...isn't that in Utah?" I asked. "Where they have that film festival?"

"Yep, it's my favorite place to ski. I used to water ski as a kid in Bayou Tail and on Lake Berg, but snow skiing is an entirely different feeling." He cleared his throat. "So, what's going on with these bodies? You said one is a kid who was fishing on our property, but who's this other person?"

"That, we don't know," I admitted. "I was hoping you might be able to help. We think the body was buried there anywhere from a few years ago to thirty years ago."

"Thirty years ago?" he echoed. "I...but I don't understand. How would a body get buried on our property? It was only my dad and mom who lived there."

I raised an eyebrow to Amy, jokingly questioning her report of a clean criminal record on Mr. and Mrs. Boudreaux. "Did your parents have any problems with neighbors over the years? Land disputes or anything?"

"No, not that I know of, but my dad's been dead for three years and the property's been vacant for all that time, so there's no way he did this."

"You're 100 percent correct that he didn't have anything to do with the murder of the young boy," I said, "but is it possible he knew something about the body that was buried on his property thirty or so years ago?"

"No way! My dad would *never* stand for something like that happening on his property. Murder? Never!" Albert spoke in an exasperated fashion. "He was a law-abiding man. He never got in trouble—not even as a kid—and he taught me not to get in trouble either. My mom was the same way. They both taught me to always do what was right and to respect authority, especially law enforcement officers, and to abide by the law. Their upbringing made an impact on me. They were hard on me and I didn't always like it, but it paid off. I've never had so much as a traffic ticket in my life. And now, I'm instilling those same values in my own children."

I glanced at Amy and raised a palm, wondering what she thought. She mouthed the words, "I believe him."

I agreed, but I was also cautious. I'd just about heard it all in my line of work. I'd encountered people who lied as naturally as they breathed air, so I knew there was a chance—although slim—that this man was playing us.

"Are you home?" I asked.

"No, I'm on the road. I'm heading to work."

"Where do you work?"

"Fairfield Brewery in Durango," he said. "I'm one of their microbiologists."

Amy had been waiting with her pen poised over the paper. She wrote the name of the company and hurried off to make the phone call. If she could speak with Albert's manager while I kept Albert on the phone, then he would make a credit alibi witness—or he would destroy Albert's alibi claim.

"Microbiologist?" I asked. "What are microbiologists doing at a brewery?"

"Most of what I do is run routine analyses on beer samples to ensure a high and consistent quality of the product. It's basically a food product and we're responsible for the safety of our consumers."

I grew genuinely interested in the topic, because I'd never heard of such a thing, and it was easy to keep him on the phone for the ten minutes Amy was gone. When she returned, she began scribbling on her notebook. I kept talking while she wrote and I began to wonder if she was writing a short story. She finally turned it so I could read what she wrote.

According to his direct supervisor, he hasn't missed a day of work, and they've been extremely busy lately. He's been working about ten hours of overtime per week for the past month and a half. He's clean.

When Albert had finished answering my latest question, I immediately changed gears. "Okay, so my partner contacted your supervisor and he confirmed that you haven't missed any work."

"Do you want to also call my wife?" he asked. "I can give you her number. I'm being honest. I've been home in Colorado and I don't know what's been going on at the property."

"Sure, just for the sake of thoroughness."

He provided his wife's number and Amy stepped out a second time.

"Look, when we were looking for the missing boys," I said while waiting for Amy to make the call, "we didn't know whose property we were on. Once we did some research and learned that your family owned it, we checked out the property map and saw that the house was included. As a precaution, do you mind if we search the house and property?"

"Sure, do whatever you think is necessary to find out who did this." I heard a blinker in the background, and figured he might have arrived at work.

"Is the house locked?"

"Yeah, but my mom should have a key. If you go to the assisted living home, you can ask for her, and she can give you a key. Her name is Tami Boudreaux. I can actually call her and let her know to expect you."

Just then, Amy returned and nodded to let me know he was clean. I thanked Albert for his time and for the permission to search the property.

"Detective, can you let me know what happens with the case?" Albert asked before we ended the call. "It's troubling to me to think there was a dead body buried on my dad's land, and I'd like to know who the victim was and who did it. I'd also like to know if my parents were ever in any danger."

"Sure thing," I promised.

CHAPTER 18

As soon as we ended the call with Albert Boudreaux, Amy and I headed straight for the assisted living center in Central Chateau Parish to meet with Tami Boudreaux. The center was a large brick building surrounded by an eight-foot metal fence. There must've been 100 or 150 apartments on the property.

We approached a shack that was manned by two armed guards. Amy and I indentified ourselves and I told the guards why we were there. After making some calls, one of the guards led us through the complex and to an apartment on the ground level.

"Mrs. Boudreaux lives in this unit," the guard said. "When you're done, please buzz the guard shack. We like to escort our guests while on the property."

I nodded and thanked the guard. When he was gone, Amy knocked on the door. We didn't have to wait long. The door opened slowly and a short lady with the purest white hair I'd ever seen peered out.

"Are you Detective Wolf?" she asked, glancing down at my pistol and badge.

"Yes, ma'am."

"Albert said you were coming to visit." She smiled and stepped back to let us in. Once we were inside, we explained why we were there and asked her about the body buried on her property. Based on her reaction, it was plain to see she knew nothing about the case. It was also plain to see that she didn't get many visitors, as she quickly made a place for Amy and me to sit and she invited us to say for lunch.

Amy led the interview. She asked questions about the Boudreaux family history, and she framed them in such a way as to elicit long responses. We wanted to know as much as we could about her family and land. Nothing was off limits and nothing was too trivial. Somehow, in some way, this case had to come back to the family.

If we were hoping to find a gold nugget of information in something Mrs. Boudreaux would say, we were sorely disappointed. An hour into the interview, we were no closer to understanding the family's possible connection to the crime than when we'd first found the body two days ago. We did learn that Albert was an only child, he played in the woods a lot as a young boy, he was once bit by a water moccasin, he didn't date much while he lived in Mechant Loup, he left home when he was eighteen, he brought two girlfriends home to visit over the years before he finally brought along the woman he would marry, and he gave her the best gift a woman could ever ask for—three beautiful grandchildren.

Amy sat there glancing at her notes. "And are you sure you've never had problems with neighbors?"

Tami chuckled and her white hair bounced as she did so. "Young lady, I might be old, but I'm not senile. I would remember having trouble with someone. And have you seen our property? We didn't have immediate neighbors, so it would be hard to get into disputes with people you can't see."

"What about strangers?" Amy probed. "Have you ever had strangers show up at the house?"

"No one just shows up to our house," Mrs. Boudreaux said. "You had to know it's there. You can't see the house from the highway and we have a gate blocking the driveway. Mark kept it chained with a padlock."

"What about people illegally hunting on your land or fishing in your little lake?"

"We did have some over the years, but the police department would come and warn them to stay away. They never came back."

"Have you ever come home and found the chain cut or the gate compromised in some way?"

"We've never had any problems at the house, which I think was the point. You see, child, Mark's father was involved in a bitter feud over land when he was a young man. It was up near Lake Charles—that's where his family is originally from—and they left the area when Mark was two years old. His father always said neighbors caused nothing but trouble. When he left Lake Charles, he searched far and wide for a place of solitude, where he could raise his family in peace. That's when he found a large stretch of land that no one else wanted, so he bought it and that's where he built the family home."

"Why didn't anyone else want the land?"

"It was shaped like a large sideways L," she explained. "The only way to reach the larger part of the L was to drive down this long, narrow and muddy road. The house is about a mile from the highway and, back then, the road was rugged and nearly impassable—at least, that's what Mr. Boudreaux told me. He said it was the perfect spot to raise his family and avoid conflict with people. When he and my mother-in-law passed away, Mark and I decided to raise our family there."

"How long ago was that?"

"Oh, we've been there for fifty years. I really love the place and wish I could still be there, but I just can't keep it up on my own. Mark wanted the property to stay in the family, but…"

Mrs. Boudreaux's voice trailed off and her face fell. When she spoke again, she sounded sad.

"Albert's our only child and we were hoping he would make it his home someday, too, but I'm afraid that day will never come. He loves living in Colorado too much and his wife really doesn't want to move down here. When she visits, all she ever does is complain about the mosquitoes and gnats."

Amy questioned her a little more, but the conversation had played itself out. Mrs. Boudreaux was genuinely disappointed when we said we had to leave, but readily surrendered keys to the house and gate.

"You can lock the door and leave the keys on the table when you're done," she said. "Albert will get them for me when he comes down for Christmas."

We thanked her and called the guard, who escorted us through the complex and out onto the street.

"Well, what do you think?" I asked Amy as we drove back to Mechant Loup.

"It's almost noon, so I think I want some Chinese food for lunch."

"That bad, eh?"

"The house and property are so secluded that no one even knows it's there." She grunted. "If someone in the family didn't do it and strangers can't even see the place, how on earth did a body end up back there?"

I didn't have an answer, so I kept my mouth shut and drove. And since we didn't have time for a sit-down meal, we picked up food from a drive-thru and headed for the Boudreaux property.

CHAPTER 19

Amy and I located the driveway that led to the Boudreaux home, but just barely. It was overgrown with weeds and the shell street had been reduced to a muddy mixture that was more slop and grass than anything else. I drove a few yards along the wet road when I realized I'd probably get stuck before even reaching the gate, so I reversed course and got out of there. Even though my Tahoe is a four-wheel-drive, I didn't have the right tires for this obstacle course.

"I'll head home to get my truck," I said. "Do you need to stop at the office?"

"What are the chances you'll find something out there?"

I shrugged. "Not good."

"If you don't mind, I'd like to check something out while you play around in the mud."

"Do I get to know what it is?"

"It might be nothing, but I was at the library once and saw a book about local mysteries. I read the dust jacket and it teased a couple of unsolved murders from Chateau and some of the other surrounding parishes." She fiddled with the end of her ponytail. "I'm wondering if this body might be related to one of those cases. From what I read, most of the murders featured in the book were never solved."

That seemed like a good idea to me, and I said as much. After crossing the Mechant Loup Bridge, I drove down Washington Avenue, dropped Amy off at the police department, and then headed home. I could hear Achilles barking long before I pulled under the carport. He used to always bark like that when he heard Susan or me approaching. It wasn't a deep and threatening bark like when he saw a stranger or a cat. Instead, it was a yelping sound that seemed to suggest he was begging us to give him some attention.

As soon as I parked, I let him out of the back yard. Coco was sleeping under a shade tree and wasn't interested in moving. I grinned. Ever since I'd brought Coco home, Achilles didn't bark as much when we drove up. He was usually preoccupied with his partner. Now that she was sleeping and ignoring him, I guess he would settle for my attention.

I rubbed his ears and asked, "Want to go for a ride?"

I'd be willing to bet he understood me, because he almost peed on himself with excitement. I walked inside to change into a pair of old jeans. I then grabbed my hip boots and a machete from the shed. I checked on Coco before leaving. She had rolled over onto her side and had a dreamy look on her face.

"Let's go, Big Man." I walked across the driveway to my truck and opened the door. I had a five-inch off-road lift on my truck, but it was no match for my large German shepherd. With a lunge, he sailed through the air and landed deftly on the driver's seat. Before I could step up on the running board, he had already moved to his position riding shotgun.

I slid his window down and he stuck his head out of the window when we hit Main Street. His tongue dangled from his mouth and his eyes squinted in delight as the wind caressed his face. I was a little envious of my dog. He had not a care in the world. Nothing to worry about. His stress level was zero.

As for me, I was starting to feel the strain of this case. I knew if something didn't break soon—if I didn't get one little nugget of hope—Red McKenzie might start killing people.

Within a few minutes, I turned onto the sloppy street. The trees on either side were thick with vegetation and stretched as far as I could see up ahead. They seemed to be closing in on the road and branches hung low. It would be a fun ride. I paused to shift my truck into four-wheel-drive. Achilles chomped excitedly, as though he knew what was about to happen. Giving it some gas, I felt the truck groan as the four tires gripped the wet mixture of mud and shells and pulled us forward. The encroaching branches slapped at my truck and I got hit in the face a few times. Achilles snapped at a few of the branches on his side, and I knew he wasn't impressed.

The going was pretty easy until we reached the gate. It was here that I pulled on my hip boots. Achilles studied me and I knew what he was thinking: *Where are my boots, asshole?*

"Sorry, Big Man, I don't have any for you."

I sunk six inches in the mud when I stepped out of my truck.

After trudging to the gate, I inspected the lock to make sure it was secure. Everything was intact, so I opened the gate and drove through the opening. My truck slid a little as we moved forward and I soon encountered a long stretch of water. The rain had definitely done a number on the road.

"Hold on," I called to my dog, as I put pressure on the accelerator. Mud and water flew into the air. Some of the slush peppered my left arm and I even took a blast to the side of my face. The rear end slid from side to side and I had to steer into the slides to keep my truck moving between the ditches. Achilles seemed to be enjoying this part as much as I was.

After jostling along the last hundred feet, we broke into a large clearing where an old wooden house stood majestically at the center of the property. The path leading up to the house was better covered. The shells were thick and the ground made a gradual ascent to the homestead.

"We're home," I said cheerfully, but Achilles wasn't fooled. I parked in the shade of a large cypress tree and stepped out of my truck. Achilles bounded out behind me and wasted no time scouring the area, his nose to the ground as he took in the new scents. He lifted his leg often and marked the property as his own. I grabbed my camera and took some wrap-around photographs of the house and property—careful not to include my dog—and then began my search.

CHAPTER 20

I searched the old barn first. It was a pole barn and the hard-packed earth was surprisingly dry. The ground area was empty except for a tractor and some other farm equipment, such as a box grater and a bush hog. A row of garden tools hung from pegs on one wall, and rope and other gear hung from pegs and nails on the opposite wall. I was about to turn away when the row of garden tools caught my eye. I wasn't sure exactly what it was at first that had gotten my attention, but something seemed off about the display of tools.

I walked to the wall and stood directly in front of it, and that's when it hit me—there was an empty peg. I checked the tools from left to right, counting them off in my head and trying to figure out what could be missing. There was a rake, a hoe, a posthole digger, an empty peg, an axe, a T-post driver, a chainsaw, and a pitchfork. I snapped my singers. The only thing that appeared missing was a shovel—and I was sure we had found it in the woods.

The hairs on the back of my neck stood up. The killers had been in this barn. I slowly scanned the shadows of the room again, making sure to look up and then under the tractor. I sighed. The room was truly empty.

There was another wooden structure behind the barn and I made my way in that direction. The door to the structure was made of weathered planks. I caught a splinter when I pulled it open. I removed it from my finger with my teeth and stepped into the small room. There were two wooden thrones—one lower than the other—and I instantly knew I was standing in an old outhouse.

It was dark inside the outhouse, so I walked back to my truck and retrieved my flashlight. Achilles was sniffing around the outhouse and I thought I saw him make a face.

"Yeah, it stinks in there," I said, reentering the small enclosure. I was sure it hadn't been used in fifty years, but the smell hadn't faded during all of that time. Light in hand, I searched every inch of the room, but other than a large water snake stretched across one of the ceiling joists, it was empty.

I walked out into the sunlight and made my way across the yard, heading for the front door of the house. Achilles had moved to an old abandoned chicken house and was pawing at the wire. He had never smelled a chicken before and I wondered if the odor still lingered. I hollered a warning for him to stay in the yard and stuck the key in the lock.

The hinges squeaked when I pushed open the door. Surprisingly, it was cool inside the house. I wasn't sure exactly what I was looking for, but I didn't waste much time. I went through all of the rooms, searched under the furniture, dug through the closets and drawers, checked behind the shower curtains, and even peered into the attic. Just like the barn, it was empty.

There were dozens of pictures displayed around the house—the walls in the hallway were literally covered in frames—and I photographed as many of them as I could. We didn't know the identity of the man we'd removed from the grave, but I wondered if it could be one of the fellows featured in a picture frame nailed to the wall.

Once I'd photographed the pictures, I decided to leave. I'd found nothing to suggest someone had been in the house recently, so I locked up and stepped out onto the porch. A warm breeze blew across the yard and rustled my hair. I stood there scanning the property. Melvin had tracked the suspects northward and the trail had ended about a mile from the gravesite. I thought back to the map Amy had pulled up of the house and property. If I was remembering correctly, I was a mile and a half from the gravesite.

I was pretty positive that the shovel we'd found at the scene would be the missing shovel from the barn, so the killers had to have come here. But had they walked through the woods or come by car?

I stomped off the porch and began searching the shells for tire tracks. The rain would've definitely washed away any tracks in the mud, but indentions in the shells might still be visible. I worked from east to west along the shell driveway, searching one square foot at a time. When I reached my truck, I found tire tracks through the shells to mark my path, but that was it. If a vehicle had come through this driveway in recent time, the tracks were gone.

"What do you think, Achilles?" I asked my dog as I ambled toward the woods. He fell in beside me and let out a groan. "You're right—there's no way they came through here, because they didn't have a key to the gate, but I do believe they walked through the woods to borrow that shovel."

I stopped at the edge of the trees and searched for a trail. "Know why you never loan people your tools?" I said to my dog. "It's because they never bring them back—and they might use them to murder people."

The undergrowth was thick in that area. If someone had walked through here recently, the rain would've covered their tracks, and it would be impossible to find any sign. Knowing I was probably wasting my time, I set off into the trees anyway.

Achilles walked beside me for a ways, but then broke away when we came to a small clearing. I paused and checked the ground. I was no tracker like Melvin. Sure, I had learned some things from him over the years, but I couldn't hold a candle to his skills. As I walked the perimeter of the clearing, I suddenly felt a tickle on the back of my neck and I shivered involuntarily. I glanced over my shoulder. Achilles was scratching at the soft mud, seemingly bored. If something was out there, he would've been on high alert. I relaxed and continued walking the perimeter.

When I reached the eastern side of the clearing, I stopped dead in my tracks. Although most of the rain water that had been dumped on the area last night had drained away, there was still some standing water heading off to the east through an opening in the trees. While it wasn't unusual for this to happen in the swamps, what was unusual was that the water was shaped like two tires tracks leading away from the clearing.

I trudged forward, my hip boots sinking in the mud, and stopped when I reached the linear tracks of water. I squatted and examined them closely. Achilles hurried over to me and sat beside me. I hooked an arm over his back and hummed to myself. I was no Melvin, but I was almost positive I was looking at tire tracks and I was almost certain they were fresh. Surely, if they had been here for more than a few days, they would've been washed away by now.

I grabbed my cell phone and Achilles walked away.

"Melvin," I said when he answered. "Want to work some overtime?"

"On Zeke McKenzie's case?"

"Yep."

"Hell, I'd work that for free."

Before I could thank him, I heard a strange noise from Achilles. I turned and saw that his snout was shoved deep in a patch of thick grass and he was sniffing aggressively. Whatever the thing was, it was concealed by the grass, which was about eight inches tall, so it couldn't be very big.

"I have to go," I told Melvin. To Achilles, I said, "What're you doing, Big Man?"

As I approached him, I noticed his hackles were up and this alarmed me. My first thought was that he'd found a snake. If it was a copperhead or a rattlesnake—the latter wasn't too common around here—he was in big trouble.

"Achilles...off!" I called as I walked toward him. He didn't seem to hear me, or he was ignoring me. This was even more alarming, because he never ignored a command.

When I reached him, I still couldn't see what was in the grass. I grabbed his collar and gave him a tug, but he resisted. "Achilles...*off!*"

The sternness in my voice must've broken through his concentration, because he reluctantly allowed himself to be dragged away. I told him to sit. He hesitated, but I didn't have to repeat the command.

Once he was on his haunches, I looked him right in the eyes and said, "Stay."

He licked his lips and glared at me, as though to say, "Kiss my ass."

"I'm not kidding, Big Man, you'd better stay right where you are—got it?"

He smacked his jowls and then lowered himself to a lying position. Satisfied he was paying attention again, I turned and walked to the spot he had been attacking with his snout. The grass was smashed where he had been sniffing and it marked the exact spot, but I couldn't see all the way to the muddy ground because the foliage was so thick.

Dropping to my knees—and hoping it wasn't a cottonmouth—I began lifting the layers of broadleaf weeds. I frowned deeply when I uncovered the object he had been sniffing.

CHAPTER 21

"What do you think?" I asked Melvin when he was standing beside me twenty minutes later.

"I definitely think the killers dropped it. Thankfully, the blood dried before the rains came, so it wasn't washed off."

"Not that," I said, glancing down at the bloody flashlight Achilles had found in the grass. I shot a thumb over my shoulder to where my dog was lounging in the shade of a large tree. "What do you think about Achilles being attracted to human blood?"

Melvin knew full well to what incident I was referring. Achilles had aggressively—excessively, even—defended Susan's life six months ago against some bad men. He had drunk deeply of human blood on that night, and I often wondered if it would change him somehow, make him dangerous to other humans. I wasn't worried about me or my family. He was as loyal as they came and would protect us with his life. No, I was worried about strangers who might stumble upon our property. I didn't like how he ignored me when he smelled human blood on that flashlight. It was as though he was so fixated on the blood that he didn't even hear me.

"He'll be fine," Melvin said with a dismissive wave of the hand. "If you're worried, have Gretchen Verdin work with him."

Gretchen was a sergeant with the Chateau Parish Sheriff's Office and she was their chief dog trainer. I liked the idea and planned to do just that.

But for now, though, we had a murder to solve, and we had just found a significant piece of evidence. The blood on the flashlight would no doubt come back to Zeke, but we had a real chance of recovering the suspect's DNA from the surface—if not from the outer surface, thanks to the rain, definitely from the batteries and battery cap. Of course, that would only help if the killer put the batteries in the flashlight. We'd also need the name of a suspect for comparison, and if I had that, I'd already be interviewing them.

As I began photographing the flashlight for recovery, Melvin started following the tire tracks from the edge of the woodlands where I'd found them and toward the west, where they disappeared into the grassy field that was located several hundred yards north of North Project Road. What I didn't know was if the tracks continued all the way to the highway or if they veered onto North Project Road. If the killers drove straight to the highway through that field, then that might explain why no one in the neighborhoods saw or heard anything suspicious. Since Westway canal curved to the east before reaching the Boudreaux property, it made sense that the killers would've accessed the highway from that area. Otherwise, they would have been forced to cut the lock on the gate to one of the wooden bridges.

After photographing the flashlight and the surrounding area with my cell phone, I told Achilles to follow me back to my Tahoe. Once there, I retrieved a few evidence bags—just in case we found additional items of evidentiary interest—and shouldered my backpack. I was turning to hit the woods again when I heard the roaring of a truck engine approaching. Achilles and I both watched as a red pickup truck rumbled through the water and pulled into the driveway. It was shiny new, red, and an F-150 XLT just like my own truck.

The sun glared off the windshield and I couldn't see who was driving until Amy dropped from the driver's seat.

"When'd you get that?" I asked, admiring her new ride.

"A few weeks ago." She reached into the bed of her truck and grabbed some rubber boots. As she changed shoes, she explained, "I traded in the Lexus I got from that piece of shit, Trevor. Every time I drove that thing, I thought about the asshole and it made me sick. I had quit driving it and it was just sitting in the garage gathering dust, until I realized I could turn it into something cool."

I nodded, but didn't say anything. Her ex-boyfriend was a sore topic, so I never responded when she mentioned him. When she was ready, we set off into the woods. I told her about the missing shovel, the flashlight, and the tire tracks while we walked.

"Damn, you should commission Achilles and put him to work," she said. "You might've never found that flashlight without him."

"No doubt. It was pretty well hidden and I had no reason to look in the grass." We had reached the clearing that led to the tire tracks and I pulled on some gloves. Amy took the camera from my backpack and shot some pictures before I recovered the flashlight. After it was recovered and secured in my backpack, I shouldered the bag again and glanced around. "Should we follow the tracks and catch up with Melvin, or do we check out the gravesite again?"

"I vote for the gravesite," Amy said. "We need to gather up those tent poles and the canopy. We might be able to salvage it."

I nodded and we set off through the woods, Achilles trailing off behind us. I glanced sideways at him, still a little worried, but he appeared to be his normal, jolly self.

CHAPTER 22

A thick layer of soft mud covered the floor of the woodlands—thanks to the recent storm—and it slowed our progress a bit. Still, we were able to cover the distance from the Boudreaux home to the gravesite in about thirty minutes.

I was happy to see that the water had receded. Other than a few puddles here and there, it had mostly drained into the surrounding lakes and bayous. I searched the ground for fresh shoe impressions, but didn't see any.

Achilles' black coat was covered in mud, but he didn't seem to care. He moved easily through the slop, leaving oversized paw prints in his wake. The tent canopy flopped in the breeze and Achilles headed in that direction, apparently curious about the movement.

Amy followed Achilles and I went directly to the grave. There was only about three inches of water left at the bottom of the hole, and most of it was concentrated on the area where the bodies had been buried. The adjacent hole we had dug to access the skeletal remains wasn't quite as deep, and it only had pockets of water scattered about the surface.

The ladder we'd placed in the hole was still in place, and I decided to get down there and give the area a thorough search. Cinching tight the straps on my hip boots, I grabbed the top rung of the ladder and descended into the hole. When I first put my weight on the ladder, it sank a few inches and then held firm.

It smelled earthy down there and it was dark. I shrugged out of my backpack and swung it around so I could reach my flashlight. I caught movement from above and looked up to see Amy standing there.

"Want me to take your backpack?" she asked.

I nodded and handed it up to her. "Did you find anything up there?"

"Nope, not a thing." She took my bag and put it on her own back. "Maybe Melvin is having better luck."

Achilles' head appeared at the edge of the hole and it looked like he wanted to come down there with me. He stepped to the very edge and whined a little, as though arguing with himself about whether or not he should jump into the hole.

"Stay," I said, which seemed to settle his inner conflict. He plopped down and contented himself with watching me.

I lowered myself to my knees, careful that the level of the water didn't rise above the top edges of my hip boots, and aimed the light into the water. I had kept the gloves on from recovering the flashlight, and I began feeling around with my fingers. When the storm had hit, we hadn't had a chance to search the ground beneath the body we'd found, and I was hoping to find something helpful.

I could hear Amy moving around on the ground level and I knew she was searching for whatever evidence she could find up there. I glanced up at Achilles at one point. He hadn't moved a muscle and his eyes were closed. I grinned to myself, wishing I could take a nap at work whenever I felt like it.

I continued feeling around in the area under which the skeletal remains had been located—even scooping out handfuls of mud to sift through—but I didn't locate a single item. Nothing at all. After I'd covered the entire area under which the body had been found, I sighed heavily and sat back on the rubber heels of my boots. During my work, I'd felt my cell phone vibrating in my pocket about a dozen times, and there was no doubt in my mind that Red had made at least half of the calls.

"Anything?" Amy called from above.

"Just a lot of slop," I said. "I'm coming up."

I rocked forward and placed the palms of my gloved hands in the slop to push myself to my feet. My left hand sank about two inches into the saturated earth and then brushed up against something that felt out of place. The object didn't feel hard, but it wasn't soft like the mud. I quickly sat back on my heels and looked at my hand. It was wet, but that was it. I tried to see into the indention I had made with my hand, but couldn't. It had already filled with black water.

"What is it?" Amy asked, apparently noticing my abrupt shift in movement. "Did you find something?"

"Don't know," I mumbled, scanning the earth around where I

was kneeling. I was kneeling on the area of earth we had dug out to access the body, and I knew there couldn't be anything buried under here. It wasn't the original grave—or was it? "What do you think the possibility is that there are more bodies out here? What if it's a mass grave of murder victims?"

Amy hesitated before answering. "I guess anything's possible, but I should hope the hell not."

I nodded and reached gingerly into the hole. Not really sure what to expect, my mind wandered a bit. Could it be a bone from another human? Or what about a root? Or maybe some buried artifact from the days when the Chitimacha Tribe occupied this area?

I probed the soft mud in the divot that my hand had created, but didn't feel anything. I pushed through the mud to the left. Nothing. I pushed through the mud to the right and felt the object again. Running my hand over the top of the object, I realized it was about four inches long by three inches wide. I wasn't sure how thick it was, so I began running my fingers down the side.

"Come on, Clint," Amy called. "The suspense is killing me."

"I can't just yank it out of the mud," I said, as I worked my hand downward along the side of the object. "Whatever it is, it's old and might be brittle."

When I had worked my fingers under it, I realized it was about an inch thick. I scowled.

"Can this be what I think it is?" I asked, scooping a large clump of mud that contained the object.

"What do you think it is?"

"Holy smokes, it is!"

CHAPTER 23

"Hey, Red, this is Clint—"

"Why the hell haven't you called me back?" demanded Red, his voice exploding with anger. "I've been calling you for hours and you wait until the end of the day to call me back?"

"I'm sorry, Red, but we've been busy." I pushed the door to my office open with my shoulder—my hands were full from holding several evidence bags and my phone—and let Achilles enter my office first. He knew the protocol. He was to go straight to the far corner, sit on a large cushion, and not interrupt me when I was speaking to people.

"There might be some developments in the case," I explained to Red, "but I can't discuss them just yet—"

"And why in the hell not? I'm the damn victim! You're supposed to keep me informed every step of the way. I'm starting to think you don't want to solve this case and you're probably thinking good riddance because Zeke was nothing but trouble for the town!"

Amy walked in behind me and started clearing off my desk so we could examine the evidence I'd found at the bottom of the hole. Once it was clear, I placed the bags on the desktop and shoved a hand in my pocket.

"Are you listening to me, Clint Wolf?"

"I am," I said slowly. "Where are you right now?"

"Huh?"

"Where are you right now?"

"Um, I'm home."

"How about I come over there and we have this conversation face-to-face?" I suggested. "I can update you on the progresses we've made and you can ask any questions you might have."

There was a long silence on the other end. "Are you…are you working Zeke's case right now?"

"Yes, I am. We just got back from the murder scene, where I found an old wallet that might help identify the skeletal remains we found in the grave."

"Wait, you found a wallet?" Red's voice grew excited. "Could it be from the murdering bastard who killed my son?"

"No, it's old. When we moved the skeletal remains during the storm, the back pocket ripped off and the wallet must've slipped out," I explained. "We found it in the hole we dug to access the remains."

"Will this help find my son's killer?"

"We're hoping so, Red—we're really hoping so."

"I…I'm gonna let you get back to work. I'm sorry for bothering you. I'm just sitting here going crazy. I feel like I need to be doing something. I need to get out the house. Maybe go for a ride or something."

"Look, I can put you in touch with a grief counselor," I said cautiously, thinking he would probably reject the offer. "The sheriff's office has an excellent victim's assistant team that—"

Red abruptly ended the call. I sat there staring at my phone. I knew what the man was going through. It was a violent rollercoaster ride of emotional terror—only there was no getting off of this ride. Unfortunately, it would last a lifetime.

I thought about calling him back, but decided against it. Everyone dealt with grief in their own way. If I tried to force a counselor on him, it would only make things worse.

"Did you have any luck at the library?" I asked, flipping on every light in my office while Amy covered my desk with butcher's paper. "You were gone most of the morning, so I figured you'd had time to read at least two books in that time."

"Maybe Lindsey, but not me." Amy was referring to our dispatcher's voracious appetite for reading. I couldn't remember a time when I didn't see Lindsey with a book. There were times when she was so engrossed in her book that the ringing phone or slamming door would scare her back to reality and she would scream like someone was attacking her.

"But every chapter dealt with a different case," Amy continued, "and I read the opening of every chapter. There were a few murders from this area—mostly in the sheriff's office's jurisdiction—but all of the bodies from those cases had been discovered."

Once the paper was taped down, I opened the evidence bag that contained the wallet. I carefully removed the wallet and placed it at the center of the paper. It was a leather wallet, single fold. It was worn and dried out. It was obvious that the aging of the leather had happened long before it had been buried in the grave, but being down there for thirty-plus years had definitely dried it out. It had been stitched at the edges upon being constructed, but those stitches had long since rotted away and the strips of leather had separated.

While it was probably a light tan color, it appeared a darker brown at the moment due to being submerged in the water.

Amy leaned over the desk in anticipation. "Do you think his driver's license is inside?"

Without answering her, I reached for the wallet and carefully unfolded it. The corner of a five-dollar bill was sticking out of the main pocket. It was sopping wet and I wondered if it was stuck to the leather. I certainly didn't want to tear the bill, so I opened the pocket wide and that's when I realized there were three more bills. In total, the wallet contained thirty-one American dollars—one twenty-dollar bill, two fives, and a one.

I spread them out carefully on the butcher's paper. Amy took a few pictures and we studied the money, searching for the series date on each of them. They were all at least thirty-one years old.

"Every date we've found so far is consistent with him being in the ground for at least thirty years," Amy mumbled from around her camera, taking one last shot before I examined the rest of the wallet.

There were two interior pockets on the wallet and I could see the edges of several cards sticking out of the pocket on the left flap. The pocket on the right flap looked empty. With the tips of my gloved fingers, I tried to grip the very edge of one of the cards and pull it out, but I couldn't break it free.

I indicated Amy's hands with a nod of my head. "Do you have nails?"

She flipped me off with both hands, exposing the short nails on her middle fingers. "Does it look like I have nails?"

I laughed and rifled through my top desk drawer until I found some nickel-plated evidence tweezers. Sliding the tips on either side of one of the cards, I gently worked it out of the pocket. It was a laminated card, so it had been well preserved. I squinted, trying to read the signature at the bottom of the card, but it was illegible. I glanced at the print atop the card.

"This is a membership card from a video store in Windrift, Utah," I said, reading in awe. I hadn't seen a video store membership card in years. "Remember when you could rent VHS tapes and DVDs from video stores?"

"I do." Amy was leaning over me, reading. She pointed to the signature line. "Too bad you can't see his name."

I placed the membership card on the butcher's paper and removed the next item from the pocket. It was a folded-up piece of paper and I had to use extreme care because it was saturated. It was yellow on the outside. I placed it on the butcher's paper and began peeling it back one layer at a time. At one point, a corner ripped and I cursed inwardly. Finally, I had unfolded it and stretched it out across the butcher's paper.

"Well, I'll be damned," I said, staring down at the Walmart receipt. I was able to make out that it was for a purchase of a Ruger GP100. It had been a lay-away transaction and he—I was presuming it was our victim—had paid a little over $300 for the revolver. I couldn't see the serial number on the receipt because it was too faded, but I already had it from the actual weapon.

"This man's a time capsule," I said. "First, the old money, then the video store membership card, and now this?"

"It's a Walmart receipt—what's so old about that? Walmart's still thriving."

"Walmart quit selling handguns nearly thirty years ago, and look at the price."

"Oh, damn," Amy said. "That is cheap."

"Yeah, they're more than double that price now." I moved the receipt to a different spot on the butcher's paper, because the first spot was now wet. I then reached for the next item in the pocket. It appeared to be a plastic card of some kind. When it was out and on the table is when I realized we'd hit pay dirt.

"No way," Amy said, crowding even closer. "That's a driver's license!"

CHAPTER 24

"His name is Bud Walker and he's from Salt Lake City," I said, reading from the driver's license. I placed it on the table so Amy could see it. I leaned back in my chair. "What in the hell is a man from Utah doing buried in the swamps of Louisiana? Isn't that like a twenty-seven-hour drive from here?"

"I don't know. I've never been there." Amy pulled the faded driver's license close to her face. "He looks like a porn star from the seventies." She turned the license and pointed to the wooly bear caterpillar on the man's upper lip. "That hairstyle was big back then, but thank God it's out of style. I'd never kiss a man with a mustache."

I ignored most of what she said. Instead, I was racking my brains trying to figure out how this man could've gotten into those woods. I reached for the license and she handed it back. I had to squint to see Bud Walker's date of birth. I wrote it in my notes and snatched up my phone to call Dr. Wong's cell. She answered right away.

"Hey, Clint, do you have another body for me?"

"No, but we might've identified the skeletal remains."

"Oh, yeah?"

I explained how we'd found the wallet and I gave her the man's name, date of birth, and address. "Do you have any contacts in the Salt Lake City area?"

"I actually do."

"Do you think you can call them and have them research their medical records to see if he's ever been treated there?"

"Absolutely," she said. "In addition to the screws in his jaw, I found evidence of an old break in his left fibula and he's also had some dental work. Now, I have to warn you, retention policies differ from place to place. If they've retained his medical records from thirty years ago and can put their hands on it, we should be able to match him up. If not…"

I hesitated. "What do you think the chances are of that happening?"

"If he was treated in a major city like Salt Lake, the chances are good. Most large hospitals retain their records longer than is required by law and they have teams of employees whose job it is to scan old medical records into their system."

I smiled. Finally, some good news. I thanked her and stood to my feet. Achilles' ears perked up.

"Stay with Aunt Amy," I said to him. "I've got to run this fellow."

As I was walking out the door, Amy began explaining to Achilles what a pornstache was.

"Don't corrupt my dog," I called over my shoulder as I walked to the dispatcher's station, but I knew it was probably too late.

Lindsey had already left for the day. Karla McBride had relieved Lindsey and she was just getting off the phone. She looked up and smiled as I approached.

I handed her my notebook and pointed to Bud Walker's name and date of birth. "Can you run this guy through NCIC and see what you can find on him? He's from Salt Lake City, Utah."

Karla nodded and her short blonde hair bounced lightly. "Sure thing. Is this about those skeletal remains found in the woods? I heard about it on the radio on my way to work."

I cursed under my breath. It would be easier to plug a hole in a protection levee with a fist than it'd be to keep gossip from leaking out in this little town. I nodded, but didn't divulge anything more. Karla, for her part, set her fingers to dancing across the keyboards.

"Want me to bring it to you when it's up?" she asked over her shoulder.

"No, I'll wait." I shifted my feet. "I'll just stand right here and pray that you find something we can use to solve this case."

"Well, I should be able to tell you—" Karla suddenly clamped her mouth shut. "Oh, wow, look at this."

I leaned over her shoulder and glanced at the computer screen. As I read the caption, my mouth fell open.

WARNING: Suspect Armed and Dangerous.

The printer on the desktop lit up like a police car running code and it started whining loudly. Seconds later, paper began shooting from the output tray. I snatched them up as fast as they appeared. Once the printer had spat out the last page, I grabbed the report and thanked Karla profusely as I headed for my office.

Achilles looked up when I entered. There was anticipation in his eyes, but I told him to settle down, that we'd be there a while longer.

"Anything good?" Amy asked.

"He's a wanted felon!" I handed her the report. "He's been on the lam for almost thirty years."

"What's the charge?" She took the report and her eyes began shifting from left to right across the page.

"Aggravated murder, aggravated robbery and aggravated sexual assault," I said.

"What's aggravated murder and aggravated robbery?" Amy's brow furrowed. "If I were a betting woman, I'd say first degree murder and armed robbery—is that right?"

"Yep, aggravated murder is basically the same as our first degree murder and aggravated robbery is similar to our armed robbery." I leaned over her shoulder and studied the report with her, wishing to have more facts about the case. However, the printout only cited a case number, a detective's name, and a phone number for more information. The bulletin, which had been issued by the Windrift Police Department, warned that officers should use extreme caution when approaching the suspect. He was categorized as armed and very dangerous.

"He's not dangerous anymore," I mumbled, walking around my desk and glancing at the time on my computer screen. It was a little after six-thirty. Most detective divisions operated between eight and five, but they all had an on-call detective. "Do you think I should call the Windrift Police Department now or wait until morning?"

"I'd call now."

I nodded and reached for my desk phone. Before I touched the handset, it buzzed. "What's up, Karla?"

"Clint, a detective from the Windrift Police Department is on the other line," she said. "She wants to know if we have Bud Walker in custody. Should I tell her anything, or do you want to handle it?"

"Huh?" I glanced curiously at Amy, who lifted her hands, confused by my expression. "How'd they even know we have him?"

"After an agency enters a wanted person into the NCIC computer, they usually get an alert from the system when an officer runs that name," she explained. "The same thing happens with stolen items and missing persons. We'll usually receive a teletype message from the originating agency asking about the inquiry, but I've never had them call us within minutes of running a name or a stolen item. From the looks of it, this guy is *really* wanted."

"What's the detective's name?" I asked.

"Leah Anderson."

I glanced down at the report. Leah Anderson was the name of the detective on the NCIC printout.

"Please put her through."

CHAPTER 25

After Amy and I exchanged greetings with her, Detective Leah Anderson asked me if we had Bud Walker in custody.

"It was my first murder case and I've been trying to catch him for thirty years." Her voice echoed through the speakerphone on my desk. "Please tell me you've got him."

"We do," I said, "but he's dead."

"Dead? How? Did he resist arrest? Was anyone else hurt?" She took a breath and apologized. "I'm sorry, I'm just really excited. I haven't heard a whisper from him since the murder happened, and my victims' families have given up on me. I've been waiting for something to break for so long that it's surreal. Okay"—she took a deep breath and exhaled—"was he killed during the arrest?"

"No, we dug him out of the ground," I explained. "He was buried in a grave in the woods down here."

"Buried?" There was a long pause. "This doesn't make any sense. Is there any indication of how long he's been in the grave?"

"Yeah, it's looks like he's been down there for thirty years. The money in his possession was from back then, as was his driver's license, and video store membership—"

"Was the money buried with him?"

Amy and I traded glances. Somehow, I got the impression we weren't talking about the same money.

"He had thirty-one dollars in his wallet and some change in his pocket, but why do I think you're referring to something else?"

"Oh, yeah, I'm talking about something else." She let out a long sigh. "He robbed an armored car in Windrift and got away with two million in unmarked bills."

My eyes widened and Amy's mouth dropped open. I even saw Achilles' ears perk up from the corner of the room. I suddenly felt the need to assure her that there hadn't been any money in the bottom of the grave.

"If two million in unmarked bills would've been down there with him, we would've definitely noticed." I drummed my fingers against my desktop. "Can you tell us more about the robbery?"

"Bud Walker was a driver for a local armored car company in the county. The company had five trucks in operation back then, and they were responsible for transferring huge loads of cash from town to town, stretching from Moab to Salt Lake City." Leah told the story as naturally as breathing, and I figured she must've repeated it thousands of times over the years. "By all accounts, Bud was a reliable worker. Very dependable and trustworthy, according to upper management at the company. He was fifty-two at the time and had worked for the company a little over twenty-five years when the robbery occurred."

Leah paused to take a breath. When she continued, the words flowed like music that had been rehearsed religiously.

"Thirty years ago almost to the day—the robbery occurred on July 13—Bud and his partner were returning from a trip to southern Utah. As was his habit, he stopped in at his favorite video store in Windrift to return a tape and get a new one. According to his partner, Winona Munday, this was routine."

"I hate to interrupt you," I said, "but his body was dug up on Monday night, which was July 13. That's thirty years to the date of your robbery."

Leah grunted. "Huh, I wonder what it means."

I apologized for interrupting and asked her to continue.

"Bud was twice married and each marriage ended in divorce. The first marriage lasted as long as it took for them to drive home from the wedding, but the second went on for ten years. They had one child together—a daughter—and they divorced when she graduated from kindergarten."

"That sucks," I muttered, considering my own daughter and how she would feel if Susan and I divorced when she turned five. It would be horrible.

"According to Winona, Bud spent most of his time watching movies. He watched them much faster than they could be produced, so he often rented the same movies over and over. She said they stopped at the video store in Windrift at least once a week for him to drop off a handful of movies and get a handful of new ones. She said he was never inside the store for more than twenty minutes, but on this day, he had been inside for at least thirty minutes when she began to get worried that they would get in trouble for taking too long."

"Were they supposed to check in when they made stops along their route?"

"They weren't allowed to make stops except for at the designated pickup points, and the video store wasn't a designated pickup point," Leah said. "They could've gotten in trouble for stopping at the video store. Winona, who was a single mother of two little girls, was afraid to get fired, so she dared not call it in. She needed her job to support her kids."

Amy grunted to let us know she understood how Winona must've felt.

"After waiting thirty minutes, Winona decided to leave the truck—a cardinal sin—to check on Bud. The company's rule is that one person must always remain in the truck, but Bud had left his radio in the truck and she couldn't reach him." She let out a chuckle that was devoid of happiness. "It's hard to imagine now, but they didn't have cell phones back in those days, so she had to leave the truck to get him."

"Yeah, I actually remember a time when we had payphones and beepers," I said longingly. "Now I'm more attached to my cell phone than I'd like to admit."

"Aren't we all?" Leah asked. "Anyway, Winona figured Bud was having a hard time making a selection, so she took the keys and hurried inside. She said there were no other vehicles in the parking lot and she hadn't seen a car pass on the highway in over ten minutes, so she figured she'd make a quick run inside to prod him along and then hurry back to the truck." Leah sighed heavily. "Boy, was she ever wrong."

CHAPTER 26

"What happened?" I asked when Leah was quiet for a long moment.

"It's probably the most gruesome crime scene I've ever visited." Leah took another deep breath. "She said that when she went through the door, she was temporarily blinded by the darkness inside the room. Once her eyes adjusted, she saw Bud standing behind the counter. She said he had a strange look in his eyes and his shirt was unbuttoned. She asked him what he was doing behind there, but he didn't answer. He just turned his gaze to the floor behind the counter. Telling him they had to hurry and get back to work, Winona walked to the counter and looked down. The first thing she noticed was that Bud was naked from the waist down. His uniform pants and underwear were down by his feet and his gun was in his hand."

"Were his uniform pants navy blue?" I asked. "The pants on our skeletal remains appeared to be navy blue."

"That's them. When Winona turned to see what Bud was looking at, she saw the video store clerk lying wide-eyed on her back. She said she thought the worker was alive and only scared, but when she didn't blink after a long moment, she knew the girl was dead. The young girl was also naked and she had three gunshot wounds to her torso—two in her left breast and one in her stomach."

"Oh, wow, our skeletal remains had four spent casings in the cylinder of his revolver," I mused aloud. "Three to your victim and one to his head, perhaps?"

"I...yeah, I mean, I guess that's possible." Leah suddenly sounded choked up. "That young girl—Rebecca was her name—she was only seventeen, you know? She was set to graduate the following year. I knew her. I'd rented from her before. This job is never easy when you're faced with a scene like that, but when it's someone you know, it's…"

Leah's voice trailed off.

"Yeah," I said softly, thinking back to the scene that had unfolded years ago when my first wife and daughter had been killed. I shuddered involuntarily. "I know what you mean. It's a heart-stopper."

"That's a good way to put it." I thought I detected a sniffle from the other end of the call, but she cleared her throat and pressed on. "Winona was frightened, as you can imagine. Her first instinct was to run out of that place screaming, but she figured it would get her shot in the back, so she stood calmly and asked Bud what was going on. He didn't say a word. He just pulled up his pants and told her they had to leave. She figured it would be safer for her if she could get outside in the public view, so she turned to walk out the door. She said she didn't see him move, but he was on her fast—before she could reach the door and before she had a chance to draw her gun."

"He attacked her?"

"Oh, yeah, he brutalized her. It was one of the more severe beatings I've seen."

"Did he sexually assault her?"

"No, he beat her to within an inch of her life. Both of her eyes were swollen shut. He broke her jaw and her nose. Her arm was fractured, three ribs cracked, and he stomped her in the groin, fracturing her pelvis. She…she said she began to think—"

Leah quit talking abruptly. After a few seconds, she apologized. "No matter how many times I tell her story, I get choked up on this part. While Bud Walker was trying to beat her to death, she wasn't thinking about herself or the trauma she was enduring. She was thinking about her girls. She was wondering who would take care of them if she died. She said she could see them at her funeral, crying and heartbroken. She didn't want to break their hearts by dying, so she decided she would live."

I sat there transfixed, frowning deeply. It was all too reminiscent of the beating Susan had taken a few months ago. The emotional wounds were all too fresh.

"What did she do?" The words that spilled from my mouth sounded like it came from someone else's voice.

"She knew that if she ever wanted to see her girls again, she would have to convince Bud to stop beating her. And the only way that would happen was if she was dead, so she died. She closed her eyes and went limp, playing dead. Although she was writhing in pain on the inside, she held her breath and kept a relaxed expression on her face. It worked. He saw her go limp and stopped a few seconds later. He hit her one last time to check for a response. That's the blow that cracked her pelvis. She said it was the most excruciating pain she'd ever endured, but she's alive today because of it."

"Wow," I said, glancing over at Amy. Her jaw was set and her fists were clinched. I knew that if Bud Walker hadn't already been dead, Amy would've quickly made it happen.

"Yeah, it was horrible," Leah said. "She was in the hospital for over a month and spent another six months in rehab. She's been seeing a therapist ever since, but the pain in her eyes has never faded."

"Do you still talk to her?"

"Every now and then she'll drop by the police department to see if we have any leads. The armored car company had put out a reward for his capture and the police department doubled it. Some business people from town also put up a separate reward, but we haven't gotten as much as a single bullshit lead. It's been complete radio silence since the day it happened."

"Was the truck left at the scene?" Amy asked, leaning forward to speak directly into the mic on the phone.

"No, it was abandoned near a canyon about twenty miles outside of town," Leah explained. "It was located three days after the murder by a couple of teenagers who were fishing in the area. It had been doused with gasoline and set afire. We might've found it earlier had it been burned near a neighborhood, but it was burned in a desolate area. There was no one around to see the smoke."

"How was the crime discovered?" Amy wanted to know.

"Well, the truck was reported missing ten minutes after four when it didn't show up at company headquarters. Since the stop at the video store was unauthorized, no one thought to check there until about five o'clock, when the owner showed up to change out the register. That's when he found Rebecca dead on the floor and Winona lying in a pool of blood, barely breathing." Leah paused to tell someone in the background to give her a minute, that she was still on the phone with the detectives from Louisiana. "If the manager had been a few hours later, he might not have made it in time. The ambulance arrived within minutes and rushed Winona to the hospital. She had already been transported by the time I arrived. I didn't get to interview her for about a week."

"Is it safe to assume your medical examiner completed a sex

crimes kit on Rebecca?" I asked, wondering how difficult crime fighting was back in those days. There had been rapid technological advances in the eighteen years since I'd first joined the ranks of law enforcement—especially in the area of DNA—and I couldn't imagine what things might have been like twelve years before that time.

"Yes," she said. "About fifteen years ago, I requested that the DNA samples from the crime scene and from the victim be entered into CODIS, but we haven't had any hits yet."

"The lab will be entering the DNA from the weapon we recovered and from tissue that was scraped from Bud's bones," I said. "Hopefully it'll match up to your case."

"God, I hope so. It would be nice to put this case to rest before I retire."

I pursed my lips, lost in thought. Finally, I asked, "Detective, do you think Bud planned this as a robbery and just killed Rebecca and tried to kill Winona as an afterthought? Or do you think his attack on Rebecca was a spur of the moment thing, done in the heat of the moment, and the robbery was the afterthought?"

"Hmm, that's a good question. I've always figured the entire ordeal was planned, from beginning to end. I also thought he must've had an accomplice, because I thought it was impossible for him to have escaped the area of the burned truck on foot. I strongly believe someone gave him a ride, especially since he lit off with two million dollars in cash. There's no way he lugged that on his back." She grunted. "Several of my colleagues argued the point, saying there was no way he had an accomplice. They argued that it's harder for two people to keep a secret than it is for one, and that it had to be a one-man operation and that the one man had kept his mouth shut. However, in light of what you've found, I'd say they were wrong. His accomplice must've gotten greedy."

"I'm sure you know the old mafia adage," I commented dryly. "Three people can keep a secret if two of them are dead."

CHAPTER 27

I had a lot of questions for Detective Leah Anderson. I began by asking her if they had developed any additional suspects.

"No, not a one. We dug deep into Bud's past, but we couldn't find a single person who might have acted in congress with him. He was living alone at the time. We investigated both of his ex-wives, his daughter, and every friend he'd ever had since grade school. Every person we interviewed—and there were hundreds—had an alibi."

I leaned back in my chair and tried to figure out what his connection to Mechant Loup might be. "In all of your interviews, did you talk to anyone from Louisiana?"

"Nope. They were all locals. I don't know if Bud ever left the area. According to his second wife, he never liked to travel. He just wanted to sit home and watch television. He liked movies and he was a sports fanatic. She said she couldn't get him out of the house on the weekends and it drove her crazy. That's part of the reason she left him. We spent years trying to figure out where a man with two million dollars would go if he never liked to travel. I guess the swamps of Louisiana are about as off-the-grid as it gets."

"What about other jobs?"

"He worked construction straight out of high school and went to work for the armored car company when he was twenty-seven," Leah said. "He never missed a shift and was always volunteering to work extra shifts. He also covered for his coworkers who had families during the holidays. By all accounts, he was a good man. I guess he just snapped."

"That's some snap." I grunted, shaking my head. A thought

suddenly occurred to me and I bolted upright in my chair. "Detective Anderson, we didn't find any money, but that doesn't mean it wasn't down in that hole. The only reason I can think of for digging up a dead guy is if there's something valuable in that hole. They didn't go down there for his gun, because it was still in his holster."

"Are you thinking they dug him up for the money?"

"Absolutely. Greed is a powerful motivator and two million in unmarked cash makes an enticing prize." I drummed my fingers on the arms of my chair. "That would mean someone from Utah drove down here with him and buried him in that grave, or someone from Louisiana went up there and helped him pull the heist. What's your best guess for a suspect from Utah?"

"I've got no idea," she said. "What about you?"

"Not a one. Whoever killed him did it thirty years ago on private property, and the owner of the property is dead, the wife is in an assisted living home, and the son has been living in Colorado for nearly forty years."

"Colorado?" Leah sounded curious. "Where in Colorado?"

"He lives in Sage County, but he works for Fairfield Brewery in Durango. His name's Albert Boudreaux."

"Hmm, there might be a connection. Want me to check him out?"

"It wouldn't hurt, but Amy spoke with his employer and his wife while I kept him on the phone. They both verified he's been home since February, so—even if he was the one who planted Bud down here—it couldn't have been him who dug up the grave."

We were all silent for a moment, Amy and I trading glances and Leah breathing lightly on the other end. Finally, I asked her if she would show me the case file if I drove to Utah. Amy's brow furrowed and she mouthed the word, "*Drive?*"

"Sure, I've never filed it away," Leah said. "It's still in my office. But...why wouldn't you fly? You could be here in four or five hours."

"I doubt our suspects would risk bringing two million in cash on an airplane." I nodded, sure of it. "They're on the road and they're probably heading back to Utah. I'd have a better chance of running into them on the road than in the air."

"Okay, I'll be expecting you. Meanwhile, I'll start going through my list of witnesses from back then and making contact with them. If any of them have been on a long road trip, it should be easy to uncover."

I glanced at the time on my computer. It was almost eight o'clock. We had been on the phone for over an hour.

"I'll head out tonight," I said, accessing the map on my computer and calculating the time and distance. "I should be there by Saturday morning."

Once we'd ended the call, Amy threw up her hands. "And what am I supposed to do?"

"Can you check with every motel, hotel, and bed and breakfast in the area to see if anyone from Utah checked in within the past two weeks?" I asked. "Now that we know there's an out-of-town link, we need to pursue that angle. Let's hope that whoever they are, they're felons and the lab will be able to match their DNA to the flashlight and shovel through CODIS."

"If this happened on Monday night, why should I go back a couple of weeks?" Amy wanted to know. "If it were me, I'd roll into town the weekend before the exhumation, get what I came for, and haul ass out of Dodge."

"You're probably right, but they might've been in town for a few days before the dig. Would you go straight to the location after thirty years of waiting, or would you put the area under surveillance first?" I waved a hand around my office. "I bet everything's changed around here in thirty years."

Amy nodded. "You have a point. I'll begin with check-out dates and work backwards from there."

I stood and donned a pair of gloves. Amy did the same and helped me secure the items from the wallet into separate evidence envelopes. Once that was done, we entered them into the evidence lockers and I told her I'd stay in touch during my trip.

"You'd better," she retorted, and led the way out into the warm evening air.

I drove straight home with Achilles and we found Susan in the gym. She was working over the heavy bag that hung at the center of the boxing ring. Sweat flew from her arms with each punch she threw. Achilles stretched out on the concrete and watched Susan with interest. We all felt at home when Susan was working her bags.

She must've sensed our presence, because she abruptly stopped and whipped around. She relaxed when she saw me standing there. She smiled and approached the ropes that surrounded the boxing ring. Draping her glistening arms over the top rope, she smiled down at us. "What's up, love?"

I shoved my hands in my pockets. "Um, I need to head to Utah. It turns out our skeletal remains belonged to a guy named Bud Walker, who was from Utah. He's a suspect in a murder and armored car heist from thirty years ago. I need to study their old case file. It might provide some leads—help us catch Zeke's killer."

Her eyebrows rose in interest. She slipped between the ropes and dropped to a seated position on the edge of the boxing ring, her feet dangling over the side. Achilles took that as an invitation to run up and lick her boxing gloves.

"When are you leaving?" she asked.

"Tonight."

"Great. I'm coming with you." She smiled warmly. "It can be a little romantic getaway."

I hesitated, but remembered that Grace was at Disney World for two weeks. A smile suddenly spread across my face.

"If driving across the country to hunt down a murdering bastard is supposed to be romantic," I said, "then I guess that's what it'll be—a romantic getaway."

CHAPTER 28

After making arrangements with Melvin to check in on our dogs, Susan and I hit the road. We drove all through the night, only stopping once for gas, and the sun was coming up just as we were driving through Dallas. Traffic was horrible. When we finally squirted through to the other side of the city, we stopped for gas and a snack. Susan drove from there while I slept, and we didn't stop again until we hit Amarillo. After stopping for a juicy steak at The Big Texan for lunch, I took over the driving again.

Amy called when we were about an hour west of Amarillo.

"What do you want first?" she asked, her voice blaring from the Tahoe's speakers. "The good news or the bad news?"

"Hit us with the bad stuff first," I said, easing into the left lane to pass an 18-wheeler. Susan reached up and lowered the blower on the a/c so we could hear her better.

"Okay, so I went to every damn hotel, motel, and bed and breakfast in Chateau, just like you asked. Not only did I check the log books for two weeks, but I went back to the middle of last month." She took a breath and huffed. "There wasn't a single person from Utah in those logs. Not only that, but there wasn't a single person from west of Texas. No one knows we're here, Clint. It's a complete mystery how this fellow ended up in the bottom of a hole, deep in the swamps of Louisiana."

"Is that the bad news?" I had been expecting something worse. "Because that's not terrible. They could've stayed elsewhere or slept in the back seat of their vehicle."

"Don't go taking a victory lap just yet," she warned. She hesitated for a long moment.

"What is it, Amy?"

"You know how you haven't heard from Red McKenzie today?"

I hadn't realized it until just then. Something in her voice told me I didn't want to hear the rest, but curiosity got the best of me. "What happened?"

"I had to arrest him."

"What?" I groaned inwardly, hoping he hadn't done something really bad. "What'd he do?"

"He got drunk and started tearing up Mitch Taylor's Corner Pub," she said apologetically. "I tried to get him to calm down, but he said some not-so-nice things about you and took a swing at me."

"What in the hell is that place turning into?" Susan asked in exasperation. "That's the second fight there this week."

"Yeah, well, I also arrested Joseph Billiot," Amy continued. "One of the locals tried to grab Red to make him calm down, but Joseph flattened him with a punch to the temple. The victim will be okay, but he wanted to press charges."

"Why'd you make the arrest?" Susan wanted to know. "Where was Baylor?"

"He got there a few minutes after I did. I was eating across the street, so that's why I beat him there. He was really pissed. He said it's the second time someone beat him to a fight." Amy laughed and then shifted gears. "So, where are y'all?"

I told her and she said she would start checking into private rentals. "I know people put their homes and camps up for rent on those vacation websites nowadays, so that might be where they stayed."

I told her it was a good idea and was about to end the call when she addressed Susan.

"How do you like Regan?"

Susan's face lit up. "I love her! She's going to be a great fit. How is she liking her job so far?"

"She loves it," Amy said. "I had to warn her that things weren't always this exciting though. I didn't want her to get the wrong impression and think we would always be busy."

Amy was right to warn Regan. While we did have our share of excitement from time to time in Mechant Loup, on most days, it was a lazy town. There were a number of outdoor activities to keep the tourists and locals busy, but our officers did find the job boring on most days. Well, except for Melvin. If it got too bad, he hit the waters and drummed up some action.

"Oh, one more thing," Amy said before hanging up. "Y'all

should know that Melvin kidnapped Achilles and Coco. He took them for a ride in the boat. He left this morning and he hasn't been back yet."

I smiled, knowing Achilles would love the ride. I worked for about a year as a swamp tour guide and Achilles had been my partner. I remembered back then when I could almost see a tear rolling down his eye when the day was over and we'd have to head back home.

We ended the call and continued on our journey. As the day drew on, we passed through Albuquerque, Farmington, Cortez, and every small town along the way. We finally rolled into Moab at about ten o'clock. We had stopped a few times for gas, and we studied every person in the parking lot of each gas station, wondering if we might've caught up to the killers.

We had also been scanning license plates since leaving Mechant Loup, but we hadn't seen a single Utah plate until we reached Dove Creek, CO, which was about an hour and a half behind us.

"Do you think we passed them on the road?" Susan asked as she pulled into a convenience store.

I had been staring at the cars driving by, wondering that very thing. "Even if we did, we'd never know it." I glanced at the GPS on the dash. We were three hours from Windrift. "Want to drive for another hour or so and then crash for the night? I'd love to see Moab in the daytime, but I want to be closer to Windrift."

Susan agreed. After fueling up, grabbing a quick bite at a local diner on a busy strip, we got back on the road. When we were an hour from the Windrift Police Department, we settled in at a hotel near the opening to a national park. The bed was comfortable and Susan was warm as she cuddled next to me. As I closed my eyes, I almost forgot about the reason for making the road trip…almost, but not quite.

CHAPTER 29

The mountainous rocks across from the hotel were glowing orange when we stepped out of the hotel early Saturday morning.

"God, it's beautiful," Susan said, staring off in the distance.

I strolled beside her and took in the beauty. "I wish we had time to explore that national park."

"We'll have to come back with Gracie."

I liked the sound of that. Wasting no more time, we sped out of the parking lot and headed west. We ate a quick breakfast in the hotel and left early. While the eggs in the hotel weren't the best I'd ever eaten, it would certainly keep me alive until lunch time.

The stretch of road we were on featured some of the most beautiful country I'd ever seen. I'd never witnessed a landscape so golden before. I could tell Susan was also in awe, because she just stared out of her window in admiration. I loved seeing her that happy.

The closer we got to Windrift, the more troubling were my thoughts. What if this trip turned out to be a colossal waste of time? How would I go about explaining this to Red McKenzie, who now sat in jail because I hadn't solved his son's murder yet? I hadn't even given it a second thought. I wanted to see the case file for myself, and I'd made an impulse decision to leave immediately and drive straight up here. But was there more to it than that? Was I being completely honest with myself?

As I cruised by a sign that welcomed us to Windrift—Population 2,564—it suddenly occurred to me why I was here. In my heart of hearts, I truly believed Zeke McKenzie's killers were in this town. And if they were here, then I didn't want to be anyplace else.

Susan pointed to a small tan-colored brick building on the left side of the road. "I think that's the police department."

I took her word for it and turned into the parking lot. It was only then that I saw a small sign in the corner that read, *Windrift Police*. The building was tiny, about the size of a rest area bathroom. The front door was made of glass and it was tinted, so we couldn't see inside.

"At least there's a Pepsi machine out front," I commented, shutting off the engine. "We'll never go thirsty."

Susan stepped from the Tahoe and stretched. As we walked to the front entrance, she said out of the corner of her mouth, "The machine is out here because it doesn't fit inside."

When we entered the tiny lobby, I realized she was actually correct. The room was barely big enough for the two chairs cramped beside each other on a wall opposite a glass window. A receptionist in a blue sundress looked up when we entered. Her smile was pleasant enough.

"You must be the detectives from Louisiana."

Susan and I each wore jeans and a Polo shirt. Since we weren't in our jurisdiction, we carried our weapons concealed. I thought we looked like everyday folk, but apparently the receptionist wasn't fooled.

"Good guess," I said. "We're here to see—"

"Leah." She smiled again. "I'll buzz her."

I turned away from the window and glanced at Susan. She was looking at me and her expression was serious.

"What's up?" I asked.

"You're not here to see some case file. You're on the hunt."

A door across from the main entrance burst open and rescued me. A woman wearing blue jeans, cowgirl boots, and a button-down shirt stood there looking at us. She was in her early fifties with blonde hair and faded blue eyes that had seen too much sorrow stood there. She smiled—it didn't erase the sadness from her eyes—and held out her hand.

"I'm Leah."

Susan and I took turns shaking hands and introducing ourselves. Leah then led us down a narrow hall to a cramped office that was barely big enough for the metal desk, single filing cabinet, and three chairs that occupied the space. Two of the chairs didn't belong, and I knew she'd dragged them in for us. We had to squeeze in so she could close the door and then we were able to sit.

From the moment I'd stepped into the office, my eyes had been fixated on a large box resting on the desk. Inside that cardboard cube might be the key to solving my case, and I couldn't wait to dive in.

Leah remained standing and began digging file folders from the box and resting them on the table. She slid one in my direction. "These are the crime scene photos."

I opened the folder and began thumbing through the pictures. Leah was right—it was a gruesome scene. The first picture was a Polaroid and it fully depicted the violence that had descended on the small establishment.

Rebecca—the young clerk who had been murdered—was lying on her back behind the counter. She was completely nude. Her skin looked like freshly fallen snow and it greatly accentuated the bloody bullet holes in her torso. She had lost a great deal of blood and, although she had a natural porcelain complexion, I was positive it had rendered her flesh a few shades lighter than its normal color.

On the ground beside Rebecca was another young woman, but this one wore a uniform that was identical to the one in which Bud Walker's skeletal remains were wrapped.

"This picture was taken by the first officer on the scene," Leah explained, looking down at the Polaroid in my hand. "He thought he was viewing a double murder scene, but then Winona moaned and he began rendering aid."

The next photo was of the same area, but Winona was no longer present in the picture. I went through every photograph in the file—handing each to Susan after I was done—and studied every detail of each of them. When I was done, and having found nothing useful, I began diving into the reports and other documents.

Leah walked out from time to time, but she remained on hand for the most part to answer our questions. I looked up when I found a transcript of an interview with a female named Katina Walker.

"Is this Bud's daughter?" I asked.

Leah frowned and nodded. "Poor girl was only twelve when her dad murdered Rebecca and disappeared with the money."

I scanned the interview. For most of it, Leah was asking Katina about the last time she'd spoken to her dad and if she knew where her dad might go if he went on a long trip. As I read, I tried to imagine what it must've been like for the young girl to hear the news about her father. I placed the transcript down and stared off. Katina would be forty-two now. She was probably married and had kids of her own. I wondered how life had turned out for her and if she ever thought about her father.

"What is it?" Susan asked when she saw me zoning out. "Did you find something?"

"I want to talk to Katina Walker." I nodded, sure of it, but there was something I had to do first. Leaving the report behind and stepping outside, I called the coroner's office and asked for Dr. Louise Wong. I was on hold for less than a minute.

"Hey, Clint, I was about to call you."

"Well, here I am."

"Turns out, it was quite easy to find the medical records on your skeleton, thanks to Mr. Bud Walker being a wanted man," she said with a chuckle. "Everyone knew his name—from receptionists to emergency room doctors to dentists in every office I called—and I got a long list of nurses and doctors who treated him years ago. Many of them were retired, but his dentist was still in business and I found one nurse who worked for the surgeon who installed the screws in his jaw."

I sighed in relief. "Were you able to positively identify him?"

"Tentatively, not positively," she said. "I've got some film coming over the wire from the hospital, an orthopedic surgeon, and his dentist. Once I compare the slides, I'm confident I'll be able to tell you with medical certainty that it's him, but—for now—I'll just say, off the record, that it's him."

That was good enough for me. I walked back inside and asked Leah if she knew where I could find Katina.

"The last contact I had with her was at her job. She's the office manager at a law firm in the city." Leah dug through the file and pulled out a notebook. After flipping through the pages, she snatched up the phone. "I'll call her and see if she's available."

Susan and I stood silently while Leah spoke with Katina Walker. When she hung up the phone, she nodded. "She's agreed to meet with us during her lunch break."

I glanced at my phone. It was almost nine. We had been at the police department for a little over two hours. "Can we see the crime scene?" I asked. "And the spot where the truck was burned?"

"We can go to the location, but the video store is no longer there," she said. "It was demolished about five years ago after sitting empty for years, and nothing was ever built on the property. It's along a stretch of road that's not well-traveled, which is why I think Bud picked that spot to make his move."

"That's fine." I nodded. "I just want to get a feel for the area. I want to see what he saw when he was out there—or whatever's left of it."

Leah led us down the hallway and through the lobby, stopping only long enough to tell the receptionist she would be on the road for the rest of the day.

CHAPTER 30

Amy was just finishing up the transport paperwork on Red McKenzie to have him sent to the Chateau Parish Detention Center when the man called to her from the jail cell.

"Detective Cooke, can I call to check on my son?" Red's words were coherent again. When she'd arrested him yesterday evening, he could barely get his name right. "He's probably worried since I didn't come home last night."

Amy put her ink pen down and strolled out of the booking room. Red's sweaty hair was plastered to his forehead and he leaned against the bars as though they were the only things keeping him upright.

"Will you behave?"

"Yes, ma'am," he said meekly.

"I'm no ma'am," Amy said, grinning. The grin quickly faded when she recognized the pain in his hollow eyes. "Just call me Amy."

She grabbed the keys to the door and let him out of the cell.

"What about me?" Joseph Billiot had stood from the bunk where he'd been sleeping. "Can I get out, too?"

"He's making a phone call," Amy said. "Go back to sleep. I'll let you know when it's time."

"Time for what?"

Amy glared at him. "When it's time for you to grow up and stop causing trouble. Red's got a good reason to be upset, but you've got none."

"No, I got no right to do what I did," Red mumbled. "I'm trying to bring my boys up right—"

He realized he'd used the plural sense of boy and broke down crying as he remembered he only had one son now. Amy put an arm on his shoulder.

"Let it all out," she said. "It won't help, but it'll feel better for a minute."

Red pinched his eyes and grunted violently. He took a breath and blew hard, trying to will the tears away. "No, I need to be strong. I need to be strong for Paulie."

Amy just stood patiently as he tried to compose himself. When he was ready, he nodded. She led the way to the booking room and let him use the phone. He called his house and she could hear Paulie's terrified and muffled voice emanating from the earpiece. Red began telling his son that he would be locked up for a few days, but for Paulie to be strong and look after himself.

"You're a man now," Red said. "You can take care of things while I'm gone." He paused while Paulie spoke. He then nodded and continued. "I know, son, I'm sorry I didn't call last night. I let you down. I swear, when I get out of this, I'll never touch another drink for as long as I live."

Amy frowned. When Red had hung up the handset, she leaned back in her chair.

"Red, look at me."

The man raised his heavy head and stared at her through his bloodshot and swollen eyes. "Yes, ma'am?"

"If I bring you home, will you swear to me that you'll stay there?"

"You would do that?"

"Will you swear to stay home?" Amy leaned forward and rested her elbows on the desk. "And I mean *stay home*—as in, don't go anywhere. Not even to the store. Like you said, Paulie's a man now and he can do the grocery shopping. I want you to stay home and out of sight. You can call me or Clint any time you want and bitch at us until this case is solved, but don't leave your house. If you swear to that and to appear in court, I'll call the judge and get a personal recognizance bond for you and bring you home right now."

"I swear it." He hesitated. "Do I have to put up any money? I don't have much, you know."

"No. I'll give you a notice to appear in court and that'll be it." Amy called the judge while Red sat there and watched her make her case. After obtaining the authorization, she completed the paperwork, gave him the notice with his court date, and then stood. "Okay, let's go."

Joseph must've seen them leave the booking room and walk

down the hall, because he began yelling for Amy to let him go.

"I didn't do anything!" he hollered. "I'll pay my fine. Please, let me go. It's not fair that he gets to go home and I don't. He's the one who started everything!"

Amy ignored him and told Lindsey she would be right back. Red's house could be accessed by boat or down a desolate swampy road that snaked along a bayou to the south. She elected to bring him home in one of the department's four-by-four pickups, because it would be faster. It took her thirty minutes to get to his house, and forty minutes to get back, thanks to her stopping to help a woman catch a puppy that darted across the street.

The woman simply wore overalls, a bra, and white shrimpers' boots. Her hair had been stabbed in place with a lead pencil.

"These damn tourists," she grumbled when Amy jumped out of the truck and snatched up the puppy for her. "If they really loved their dogs, they'd take better care of them."

"Oh, I thought it was your puppy."

She shook her head and roughly blew hair out of her eyes. "Nah, it's for one of my renters. They came in last night and have already been a pain in the ass."

Amy nodded and stared toward the bayou, where several faded camps nestled together under large oak trees at the water's edge. It was a secluded area and each camp had about fifty feet of space between them.

"You rent to people from all over the country?"

"No, I rent to people from all over the world." She took the puppy from Amy. "I had a couple from Australia here last month, and another group from England."

"What about Utah?" Amy asked slowly.

"Sure, I've hosted people from Utah before."

"Recently?

"I...I think so." She cocked her head to the side. "Why do you ask?"

"Well, a couple of guys from Utah started trouble between two locals the other day," she explained, fudging a little. "They paid one of the locals to punch the other one and a big fight broke out."

"Do you know their names?"

"No," Amy admitted. "I just know they're possibly from Utah and they might've stayed at a vacation home here in Mechant Loup."

"Well, I can check my records when I have a minute," the woman said. "Give me your card. Right now, I need to get this puppy back to her rightful owners."

Amy gave the woman a card and asked for her name before she hurried off.

"Lucille," the woman called over her shoulder. "Lucille Cheramie."

When Amy got back to the police station, she pulled Joseph Billiot into the booking room to process the paperwork to have him transported to the detention center.

"Are you gonna let me go, too?"

She studied him for a long moment. "It depends. If you promise to go home and stay away from the bars for the rest of the week, I'll get a PR bond authorized and bring you home."

He let out a long sigh. "Yeah, yeah, I promise. I'll do whatever you tell me to do. I just don't want to go to the Chateau Jail."

Amy contacted the judge again and obtained the authorization. She then completed the necessary paperwork.

"You need to stop hitting people," Amy admonished. "These misdemeanor charges are going to start adding up and the judge will get tired of seeing your ugly mug in court. You'll find yourself pulling a long stint in the parish jail."

"But that dude grabbed Red and tried to take him down," Joseph protested. "Red's son just died. I couldn't let that man do that to him. I didn't even know the guy. He wasn't a regular, so he had no business doing that to Red."

"Regardless, if it doesn't involve you, then don't involve yourself." Amy slid the notice across the desk. "Sign here affirming you'll appear in court on that date."

"And if I don't?"

"Get your ass back in the cell." Amy stood abruptly and was about to walk around the desk to grab Joseph by the nape of his neck when he yelped.

"No, no, no...please!" He clasped his hands together like a child begging not to get spanked. "I'll sign it."

Amy sighed and took her seat as Joseph picked up the pen and affixed his signature to the document. Amy tore the notice from the book and handed it to him.

"If you don't show up in court on that date, a warrant will be issued for your arrest."

Joseph folded the notice and shoved it in his shirt pocket. "While I'm here, can I pick up my Benjamin Franklin?"

"Huh?" Amy scrunched her face in confusion. "Pick up who?"

"The chief—Chief Susan—she took a Benjamin off of me and I want it back," Joseph explained. "The man I hit from New Orleans doesn't want to press charges anymore, so I figured I could get my money back."

"Are you talking about that fight from Tuesday?"

"Yes, ma'am."

"I'll have to check with Chief Wolf before giving it back, and she's out of town right now." Amy started to stand, but Joseph remained seated.

"Can you call her and ask her?" he pleaded. "I really need the money. My rent is due Monday."

"If you don't have enough money for rent, then why are you sucking it up at the bars?" Amy shoved a fist onto her hip.

"My buddies were buying me drinks. I didn't spend a cent."

Amy begrudgingly led him to the lobby and instructed him to wait while she called Susan, who verified that the victim had dropped the charges.

"You can give him back the money," Susan said. "It's in one of the evidence lockers. I'm not sure which one, but you can check the log book. If you don't mind, just make a photo copy of it before releasing it."

Amy agreed and then asked how things were going in Utah.

"We're at the scene of the murder right now," she said. "Clint's looking around. He thinks the killers came back to Utah, but we still don't know anything."

After a brief conversation, they ended the call and Amy went to the evidence log book. She found the entry and went to the corresponding locker. She typed in her code and opened the locker, where she found an evidence envelope secured inside.

She freed Benjamin Franklin from the envelope and made a copy in the dispatcher's station. Before meeting Joseph in the lobby, she sat at a table in the radio room and began preparing a receipt. Lindsey was leaning far back in her chair reading a book, and hadn't paid any attention to her.

Amy jotted down the denomination of the bill, recorded the serial number, and was about to complete the receipt when she saw the series date.

"No way!" she hollered, jumping to her feet. The chair she had been sitting on skidded backward across the floor and crashed into the far wall. The noise and motion scared Lindsey so bad that the dispatcher screamed and fell out of her chair.

"What in the hell is going on?" Lindsey asked in a voice that was clearly shaken as she scrambled to untangle herself from the floor and find her book.

Amy laughed so hard she nearly tore her gut. Once she'd calmed down, she pointed to the one-hundred-dollar bill. "Look at the series date on that bill—it's from thirty years ago!"

CHAPTER 31

I shook my head and motioned to Leah that I was ready to leave the original crime scene. The video store where the murder occurred had been reduced to a flat piece of bare concrete surrounded by tall weeds and building debris. Other than providing some insight into how secluded the location had been, the visit served no purpose.

Susan and I followed Leah down winding backcountry roads, some of which were rugged and unpaved. Leah drove a white F-250 4x4 with a green and gold badge on the front doors and the name of her police department displayed boldly on all four sides. There were clumps of red mud stuck to the undercarriage and all four wheel wells, and Susan and I spent most of the trip in a reddish haze kicked up by her all-terrain tires.

We took so many different turns on nameless back roads that I was completely discombobulated after a few minutes of driving. Had it not been for the sun above, I would not have been able to begin to find north.

We finally turned down a rough gravel road that descended into a canyon. After jostling along for about three miles, Leah pulled off the road to the right and parked near a gnarled juniper tree. We parked beside her and met in the shade of the large tree. A narrow stream flowed lazily through the area. It was hot and I longed to immerse myself in the clear water.

"This is it," Leah announced. "This is where we found the armored truck. It was burned to the rims. Arson investigators didn't find any evidence of the leather bags or bodies in the vehicle. This is where the trail went cold."

I frowned. I don't know what I expected to find in this spot after thirty years, but there wasn't even a hint of a fire ever having taken place here.

I shot a thumb over my shoulder. "There's no way he walked out of here carrying two million dollars."

"That's what we surmised," Leah said. "We're pretty sure someone picked him up."

"Or...he could've parked a vehicle in this spot and driven himself out of the canyon," Susan offered, moving to higher ground and looking around. She put her hand to her forehead to shade her eyes from the sun. Pointing off in the distance, she asked, "What's out in that direction?"

Leah and I joined her. There were faded trails crisscrossing along the canyon floor and I could see what looked like homesteads off in the distance. From where we stood, they looked like match boxes.

"Most of those residents weren't here thirty years ago," Leah explained. "About half of the homes in this canyon back then were vacation rentals. Now, it's about seventy-five percent."

"Did y'all canvass that area?" I asked.

"Yeah. After finding the truck, we knocked on every door in this canyon and interviewed every person we could find, but no one saw anything. A couple of kids claim they saw smoke, but they pointed in the wrong direction, so we never did believe them."

I remembered seeing several canvass sheets when I was going through the file earlier. I had breezed over the names, but nothing stood out. I certainly didn't expect to recognize any of the names, so it had been no surprise. A thought suddenly came to mind.

"Hold up—wasn't Bud Walker the focus of your investigation back then?"

She nodded, her brow furrowing. "Yeah, he was the sole focus of our investigation."

"We now know he had a double-crossing accomplice." I began pacing back and forth along the creek. "We need to look at every name you interviewed from back then—in particular, all the people who lived over there." I pointed across the canyon. "If I lived out here and I was planning a heist, this is where I would bring the armored truck. I'd never have to get back on one of the main roads, which would be crawling with police. I could leave my vehicle parked right here during the heist. Once I brought the truck here, I could load up the money and drive straight across the canyon. I could hole up at my homestead and tell you I didn't see anything when you arrived to canvass the area."

Leah's face turned pale. "You think I screwed up? You think I should've looked at these people harder?"

"No, we're supposed to follow the evidence," I said quickly. "Back then, the evidence pointed to an inside job and Bud Walker was your primary suspect. You had no reason or right to search every homestead in this area. You did the best you could with the facts at your disposal."

"I appreciate you saying that, but it doesn't make me feel any better."

I approached her and looked her in the eyes. "I don't believe in luck, but had it not been for a fortuitous discovery in our swamps, we wouldn't be standing here right now. I'd be driving back and forth in front of those woods, never knowing there was a body buried there. As for you, you would've retired never knowing what happened to Bud Walker. But here we are, so let's not look back except to dig for more evidence. From here on out, we're moving forward and we're going to find whoever did this."

"Okay." She nodded. "I know you're right."

"After we meet with Katina Walker, I'd like to interview Winona Munday," I said. "I want to provide her with a list of names of everyone you interviewed back then who lives in this area—see if any of those names stick out to her. She might be the key to breaking this whole thing wide open."

Susan was chewing on her lower lip like she did when she was thinking.

"What is it, Sue?" I asked.

"What if Winona's family went after Bud Walker and exacted revenge on him?"

"Nah," Leah said, shaking her head. "Winona doesn't have any family around here. She's originally from Virginia and she ran away from home when she was little. Her father was abusive. She left to get away from him. She said she hasn't had contact with them since she left. She was terrified of her dad and said she didn't want him to ever find out where she lived. Thank God she didn't die, because her children would've had no one to care for them and would've ended up in state custody."

"What about the children's father?" I asked.

"He was a real winner. He began abusing her immediately after the babies were born. She decided she wasn't going to stick around for that nonsense." Leah paused and asked about Zeke's dad. "How's he holding up?"

"Not good."

"I guess not. I couldn't imagine ever losing one of my kids."

Leah kicked at a rock. "How old was the boy?"

"Fourteen." I paused and shifted my eyes downward and stared at my boots, considering Zeke McKenzie and my first daughter, Abigail. Had Abigail not been killed, she would've been fourteen in October. I frowned. "It's sad that a young boy had to die just so this secret could be unearthed. It's sad that any kid has to die—ever."

Susan could sense that I was thinking about more than Zeke, and she gave my hand a squeeze.

"Are you ready to go catch these assholes?" she asked.

I nodded and walked briskly to my Tahoe. My jaw burned and my chest ached.

CHAPTER 32

"Damn it, Clint," Amy grumbled, "answer your phone!"

She had called Clint fifteen times and the call had gone straight to voicemail each time. She'd left a message every time and even sent a picture of the hundred dollar bill, but he hadn't called back yet. Finally, she gave up and secured the money back in the evidence locker.

"Let's go," she said to Joseph Billiot when she threw the door open to the lobby.

He looked up, surprised. "Where's my money?"

"You're not getting the money back," she said abruptly. "Let's go—follow me."

He turned to stare at the exit. "I thought you were bringing me home."

"You need to answer some questions about that money first."

"What…what kind of questions?"

"If you'll get off your ass and follow me inside, you'll find out."

He hesitated a moment more, but then nodded and stood to his feet. "Am I in trouble?"

"It depends—did you kill Red's son?"

Joseph recoiled in horror. "Dear God, no! I would never! Red's a friend of mine. I would never do anything to hurt him or his boys."

"Do you want to help me find the person who did it?"

He shifted his feet. "Sure, but I don't know nothing about his murder. I don't know how I could help."

"You can help by telling me everything you know about the man who gave you that Benjamin."

Realization slowly spread across Joseph's face. "Oh, no! Do you think they killed Zeke?"

"You're wasting my time, Joseph." Amy stepped back and pointed down the hallway toward the interview rooms. "Get in there so we can talk."

Joseph did as directed and they were soon sitting across from each other in the interview room.

"I need you to tell me everything you know about the man who gave you that money." Amy leaned forward, staring at him with menacing eyes. "And I mean *everything*."

Joseph let out an audible gulp. "I...I don't really know anything. Like I told the chief, they might've mentioned their names earlier in the conversation, but I don't remember."

"You told Chief Wolf that there were two men," Amy said, going over the report of the bar fight from Monday, "and one of them was around seventy years of age."

"Yes, ma'am."

"How old was the other one?"

"I'm not real good at age."

"Make your best guess."

"If I had to bet on it, I'd say about fifty."

"I need you to think real hard about their names."

Joseph grunted. "I mean, I know they must've said it, but I was pretty lit, so I don't know if I would remember."

"Look," Amy said, stabbing at the desk with her index finger. "This is important. These men might've killed Red's boy."

"I mean, do you really think so? They didn't seem like the type to go murdering little—"

"Oh, so you're a detective now?" Amy's tone was mocking. "You know about these things?"

"No, ma'am, I just thought—"

"I don't want you thinking unless you're thinking about their names."

"Well, one of them might've called the other one Jim or Jimmy."

"Jim or Jimmy?" Amy wrote it down. "Was that the older one or the younger one?"

"The younger one." He rubbed his thick face. "I don't know for sure, but I kinda got the sense that they were related. Like, maybe the older guy was his dad?"

Amy tapped her ink pen against the pad. "And you never heard the younger one call the older man by a name?"

"No, I don't think so."

"Did you tell them your name?"

"Yeah, I did."

"Close your eyes and think back to that morning."

Joseph blinked.

"I'm not kidding—close your eyes." Once his eyes were closed, Amy continued. "Okay, do you see the two men in your head?"

"Yeah."

"Describe them."

"The old man's bald. He has strings of white hair on the sides of his head and on the back. He has a short, white mustache. He has little bags under his eyes and he's got a turkey neck. He's a big man, though—a little bigger than me."

"How much do you weigh?"

"Two-ninety. He probably weighs 300 pounds and he's about six-foot tall."

"Describe the younger guy."

"He was smaller than the older man—probably about two-hundred and fifty pounds, five-eleven—and he had more hair, but it was receding. It was long, too, like down to his shoulder. He had a white goatee and his nose was crooked."

"And his name was Jim or Jimmy?"

"Yes, ma'am, I think so."

"And the old man—what was his name?"

Joseph opened his eyes. "I don't know."

"Okay. Can you remember anything else? Did they mention where they were staying or where they were going? Did they say why they were here? Did they tell you when they got into town and when they were leaving? Anything at all?"

Joseph began shaking his head from the first question and shook it continuously throughout all of the questions.

Amy sighed. "Well, you ain't much help."

"Hey, I tried!" Joseph sat there watching Amy for a long moment. Finally, he asked if he could take Benjamin Franklin and go home.

"Nope, he's staying with me." Amy stood and escorted him out of the office. "I appreciate you talking with me. I'll call if I need anything more."

"Um…" Joseph hesitated in the lobby, shifting his feet nervously.

"Um what?" Amy asked impatiently.

"Can I have your number?" His face flushed and he averted his eyes from Amy's glare.

"You most definitely cannot. Now get the hell out of here before I change my mind about your PR bond."

CHAPTER 33

Amy told Lindsey she would be back later and headed out the door. She drove straight to Lucille Cheramie's compound and parked under a large oak tree. She strolled up an uneven sidewalk that was broken in places because of large roots jutting up from the ground. The entire front yard was shaded and it served as a nice reprieve from the heat.

Once Amy reached the end of the sidewalk, she made her way up a ramp that led to a screened-in porch. Not wanting to invade the woman's privacy, Amy stood outside of the porch and knocked on the screen door. She only had to wait a few seconds.

"Oh, hey, Detective Cooke, come on in." Lucille hurried to the door and held it open for Amy.

"Please, call me Amy."

"Okay, Amy, come on in." Lucille led the way into a crowded kitchen that smelled of fried seafood and fresh-cooked rice. "I didn't have a chance to look at my records yet, but let me get my book."

It was almost noon and Amy's stomach was growling. There was a huge pot of rice on the stove. A crowded tray of fried shrimp, fish, and oysters was on the table. A young girl rushed in and grabbed the tray of seafood. She smiled as she brushed by Amy and headed out the door.

Amy moved to a vantage point where she could track the girl's movements. She was heading for a group of picnic tables set up along the bayou side. There must've been a dozen tables, and nearly every space on every bench was occupied.

"Damn," Amy muttered, "they've got a lot of business out here."

"Yes, we do," Lucille said, suddenly appearing from the back of the house carrying a worn notebook. "It never gets boring here during the summer."

"If you keep cooking food like that, they'll keep coming—that's for sure." Amy took a seat at the table next to Lucille and watched as she opened her book.

"Let's see…" Lucille began humming as she flipped through the pages. Her crooked index finger moved from the top of the page to the bottom. She shook her head and turned to the next page. She did this for a few pages and then stopped. "Okay, the last people who stayed here from Utah were Jim and Jimmy. They actually checked out on Wednesday."

"Jim and Jimmy?"

Lucille cocked her head to the side and scanned the page carefully. "Yeah, that's what they said their names were."

"What were their last names?"

"They never said, but I think they were father and son."

"How can they rent from you without giving their full names?"

"As long as they pay up front and leave a damage deposit, I'd call them King James if they wanted."

"What about a credit card? Do you have that on file?"

She shook her head. "No, these men paid with cash."

"Cash?"

"Yeah, look here." Lucille pointed to the notes. Sure enough, it read, *Cash, paid in full.*

"Do people often pay with cash?"

"Not often, but I get a few each year. I don't question their reasons, I just take their money."

Amy leaned back in the wooden chair, the slats creaking under her weight. "Can I see the cash they gave you?"

Lucille eyed Amy suspiciously. "And why would you want to do that?"

Amy explained that the money might have been taken in a heist from thirty years ago. This seemed to satisfy Lucille. She left the kitchen again. When she returned, she had a money bag in tow that seemed to be busting at the seams.

Amy groaned inwardly when she saw the stuffed bag. She didn't have time to sift through stacks of cash. She needed to get in touch with Clint as soon as possible—if he would ever answer his damn phone.

"I keep proof of everything," Lucille explained when she unzipped the bag and a mountain of receipts spilled out onto the table. "You never know when something'll break down."

"I know what you mean." Amy was relieved. She watched as Lucille removed a paper envelope that was filled with cash and handed it to her.

"This is it. Lucky for you, I haven't made it to the bank yet."

Amy lifted the flap and examined the stack of bills. Most were twenties, but there were also tens and fives and a couple of hundreds. Some bills were in good shape while some were crumpled, but none of them were dated more than five years ago. "How much money is this?"

"Twenty-five hundred."

"How long did they stay here?"

"Five nights."

"So, from Friday night to Tuesday night?"

"Yes."

"And you charge $500 per night?"

Lucille nodded.

"No taxes?"

Lucille smiled and cocked her head. "Are you working for the IRS now?"

"No." Amy chuckled. "Not at all. I'm just wondering."

"When my customers choose to pay cash, I choose to have a momentary lapse of memory where the IRS is concerned." Lucille huffed. "They take too much of my money as it is. I swear, if it wouldn't be for federal, state, and local taxes, I would have everything paid off and I'd be living on easy bayou right now."

Amy nodded and placed the money back in the bag. Discouraged that she had wasted valuable time, she was just standing to leave when the young worker returned with the same tray, except it was now empty.

"Daisy," Lucille said, "do you remember those two men from Utah who stayed in Camp Pelican?"

Daisy's face lit up. "Oh, yeah, I remember them."

Curious, Amy asked if there was something special about them.

"They gave me a big tip when they checked out."

Amy suddenly grew excited. When the suspects first rolled into town, they hadn't accessed the gravesite yet and wouldn't have been in possession of the thirty-year-old money. But when they left…

"Do you still have the cash they gave you?"

"Yes, ma'am!" The girl nodded excitedly. "Want me to get it?"

"Sure."

Daisy put the tray on the counter and hurried into one of the back rooms. When she returned, she handed Amy two one-hundred-dollar bills. They looked as crisp as the Benjamin Franklin that Joseph Billiot had in his possession. When Amy checked the series date, they were identical.

"This is it," Amy said. "This is from the heist."

Daisy's face fell and she glanced from Amy to Lucille. "What's the matter with my money? I can't have it?"

Amy's heart fell as she studied the young girl. Daisy looked like a child who'd just had her favorite Christmas present wrenched from her hands and thrown into the trash.

"This money is part of a major case that we're working," Amy explained. "It's stolen property, but it's not your fault, so here's what I'm going to do—I'm going to swap these bills for two clean one-hundred-dollar bills, and I'm going to throw in an extra fifty for your troubles."

Daisy's face lit up again and she bounced up and down. "Thank you so much!"

"What're you doing with that much cash on hand?" blurted Lucille.

"I just bought a badass truck," Amy explained with a smile, "and I got cash back for my trade-in, which was even more badass."

Lucille apologized for prying, but Amy waved her off. Amy then hurried to the truck to get the girl's money. Once she'd made good on her promise, she asked Lucille if she saw what Jim and Jimmy were driving.

"It was a dark gray Silverado," she said. "A four-by-four. I noticed one of the tires was different from the others and it was missing a hubcap."

"Do you remember which tire it was?"

"No."

Amy nodded and thanked Lucille. As she hurried to the department truck parked under the oak tree, she dialed Clint's phone again.

CHAPTER 34

Susan and I parked in a space next to Leah and followed her down a sidewalk that stood in the shade of the high rise buildings on either side of us. I'd never been to Salt Lake City before and was surprised to see the skyscrapers. I had figured it for a smaller city— like Gatlinburg—but I was wrong. It was a large city surrounded by beautiful snow-capped mountains, which also surprised me.

"How can you have snow in July?" I asked Leah as we approached a row of umbrella-covered tables on the sidewalk.

"It doesn't happen often," she explained, "but we sometimes get snow up in the mountains during the summer."

"It's beautiful," Susan said.

We walked along the sidewalk and Leah pointed to one of the tables at the end of the row. A lady with dark features sat alone eating a club sandwich. She wore a business suit and had a white napkin in her lap. She looked up as we approached and frowned when she saw Leah.

"Hello, Detective Anderson." I detected a hint of hostility in her tone. She glanced at me and Susan and nodded a greeting.

"Hey, Katina, these are the detectives I told you about," Leah explained. "I'll go ahead and leave you guys alone to talk."

My brows furrowed as I cast a curious glance in Leah's direction, but she gave me a reassuring nod. As she turned to walk away, I thought I heard Katina call her a bitch under her breath.

"May we sit?" I asked, to which Katina nodded.

I sat to Katina's left and Susan sat beside me. After placing my case file on the table in front of me, I told her who we were and where we were from.

"Do you know why we're here?" I asked.

Katina set her sandwich down and wiped her mouth with the napkin. "I imagine it has something to do with my father."

"Yes, ma'am, it does." I took a breath and exhaled slowly, trying to decide how best to break the news to her. "Do you believe your father did what they accused him of doing?"

"I really don't know what to think." She shook her head and sighed heavily. "I was five when my mom divorced him and twelve when the heist happened. What I remembered of him was that he was a good and caring man. He was never mean to me or to anyone around me. I know it sounds cliché, but I never would've guessed that he'd do something like that."

"Well, I don't think he acted alone, that's for sure."

"What do you mean?"

"We have some news about your father, and I'm afraid it's not good news."

"Okay…" Her voice trailed off and she seemed to brace herself for the worst.

"During an investigation for a missing teenager in Louisiana, we stumbled upon an old grave." I paused to let that information sink in. "When we excavated the gravesite, we located the skeletal remains of a man wearing a uniform and a gun belt. There was a wallet down there with him, and in that wallet was your dad's driver's license."

Katina blinked several times and stared through me for a long moment. Finally, she settled into her chair, her shoulders drooping. "Are you sure?"

I reached for the file and dug out the driver's license. I slid it across the table and watched as she picked it up with trembling hands. Tears began streaming down her face.

"Oh, wow, this is exactly how he looked when I saw him last. It's like he hasn't aged at all." She scrubbed at her cheeks. As she stared down at the driver's license, her face suddenly scrunched up. "Wait a minute—this driver's license is old. It's from when he went missing."

"Yes, ma'am," I said softly. "He was apparently killed thirty years ago—shot in the head—and then buried in a deep hole in the swamps of Mechant Loup."

"But…but who killed him?"

"That's what we're trying to figure out," I explained. "He either had an accomplice who double-crossed him, or someone found out he had the money and killed him for it."

"So, he didn't steal the money and leave the country like the media was saying?" Her face softened and I thought I saw a smile tugging at the corners of her mouth. "I knew he would never abandon me. My mom put him down and said that was just like him, but I knew he loved me and I knew if he stole a lot of money, he would make sure I had some. He used to say he would buy Disney World for me someday when he was rich. If he really stole the money, that's exactly what he would've tried to do."

Susan and I sat there quietly as Katina spent the next ten minutes or so reminiscing about her father. Finally, she took a cleansing breath and exhaled. "I don't understand it, but I feel like a weight has been lifted off of my shoulders. My dad didn't abandon me after all. In my heart, I always knew that he would have gotten a message to me if he could have. I knew he loved me, and you've helped to prove that." She smiled warmly and looked at me with glassy eyes. "Thank you for this. It means the world to me."

As I looked into Katina's eyes, I thought back to the horrific crime scene photos I'd seen earlier in the day, and I wondered would she think so highly of her father had she also seen them. Instead of saying anything, I smiled back and thanked her for her time.

"Will I get to bury him?" she asked quickly. "Will I get to claim his body and be able to give him a proper send off?"

"In time, yes," I said. "We still have some investigative work to do and it'll be quite some time before we're done, but you'll be able to bring his body back home and give him a proper burial."

She thanked us again and then Susan and I walked away.

"Poor thing," Susan said in a low voice. "I couldn't imagine being the daughter of such an animal."

"Let's pray she never fully understands the evil that was her father," I said. "I don't think she'd be able to live with herself knowing she came from that kind of a monster."

CHAPTER 35

Susan and I met up with Leah and we began walking back to where our vehicles were parked. I was explaining what happened with Katina when my cell phone rang.

"Hello, this is Clint—"

"Where in the hell have you been?" hollered Amy.

"I'm in Utah," I explained, confused. "I told you I was leaving."

"I've been calling you all morning."

I pulled my phone from my ear and checked for missed calls. There were none. I then noticed I had over a dozen voice messages. "Oh, damn," I said after putting the phone back to my ear. "We must've been in a dead zone when we visited the crime scenes."

"You know the Benjamin Franklin that Susan recovered from Joseph Billiot—the one the tourist paid him to hit that man from New Orleans?"

"Yeah," I said, my curiosity mounting.

"It's thirty years old and it's crisp," Amy announced. "It's part of the loot from that armored car heist."

I stopped walking. "What?"

"Yep, the suspects were in Mitch Taylor's Corner Pub on Tuesday, the same day they checked out of one of Lucille Cheramie's camps," she explained hurriedly. "And get this—they also gave Lucille's helper two one-hundred-dollar bills from the same date series."

"Who are they?"

"I don't know."

"But I thought you just said they rented a camp from Lucille Cheramie?" I'd heard Lucille's name before, but I'd never met her.

"How can she not know their names?"

"They paid with cash and said their names were Jim and Jimmy. She thinks they were father and son. They're driving a dark gray, four-by-four Silverado with one tire that's missing a hubcap." She took a breath. "They probably made it back to Utah by now."

I started walking again. "Amy, there're probably thousands of dark gray Silverado four-by-four trucks with a missing hubcap. I need something more."

"Well, you'll have to work with that for now," she said bluntly. "I'll spend the rest of the day going up and down Washington Avenue pulling surveillance footage from Tuesday. We're bound to capture their faces on video."

"Faces won't help much," I said. "I need some names."

"I'll do what I can."

"Thanks. Call me when you know more."

"Yeah, well, answer your phone."

Before I could respond, she ended the call. I shook my head and updated Susan and Leah, who had both been watching me with great curiosity.

"I didn't see the names Jim or Jimmy in the file," I said. "Did I miss it?"

Leah shook her head. "Those names have never come up during the investigation."

"Any thoughts on the dark gray Silverado?" I asked.

"Same as you—there are thousands of them."

When we reached our vehicles, Susan and I climbed into my Tahoe and we followed Leah. She had called Winona at her work number and learned that she had retired. She then called Winona's cell phone and got an answer. Winona had agreed to meet with us at two o'clock, and that gave us about an hour for lunch. We were all hungry, so we welcomed the break.

"Where do you guys want to eat?" Leah asked. "We've got some good seafood restaurants in the city."

"We're from Louisiana," I said, smiling, "no one does seafood better than we do. How about some Mexican food? I thought I saw a sign for something called the Red Iguana up the street."

Leah smiled. "It's to die for."

CHAPTER 36

After a hearty meal that left me wanting a nap, Susan and I followed Leah to the outskirts of Windrift near the foot of a mountain range. She pulled into a crowded neighborhood and stopped in front of a modest home that was squeezed between two other homes.

"That's a cute little house," Susan said as we prepared to step out of my Tahoe. "I love the little garden out front."

The entire front yard was a garden and it was well manicured. There were freshly planted flowers arranged in symmetrical patterns in the small space between what appeared to be her driveway and the neighbor's driveway.

We were parked on the street and I had to duck under some tree branches as I walked to the narrow driveway. The door opened before we made it to the front porch and a woman stepped out to greet us. She rubbed her hands nervously on her jeans.

"Hey, Detective Anderson, do you have some good news?"

Leah frowned and glanced over at me. "Winona, these detectives—Clint and Susan Wolf—drove all the way from Louisiana. They have some news for you, and I'd like you to look at some names."

The woman nodded and stepped forward to shake hands. She had shoulder-length hair that was dark brown and curly. Her hand was cold and soft.

"I hear you retired," I said as we followed her into the house. She wasn't wearing shoes and her bare feet slapped gently against the floor.

"Yeah, I left the company last year." She indicated the chairs with a wave of her hand and we all took a seat. "It's hard to believe this day has come."

I noticed several cardboard boxes scattered about the living room and there were dishes on the counter wrapped in newspaper.

"Are you moving?" I asked.

"Yeah, you guys got here just in time." She took a breath. It sounded as though she had been working hard. "After I retired and my girls moved out, I realized there was nothing in Windrift that was holding me back, so I decided to move closer to them. One lives in Albuquerque and the other lives in Fort Worth. I was trying to find a centrally-located spot, and settled on Roswell. I've always been interested in aliens, so why not move there, right?"

We all made small talk, trying to break the ice, and I decided to get down to business. "As I'm sure you've probably figured out," I began, "there's been a development with the case."

Winona excused herself and walked to the kitchen to get a glass of water. She offered us a drink, but we all declined. When she was seated again, she said, "This case has taken a real toll on my life. After the robbery, I couldn't drive armored trucks anymore. I was going to quit, but the company convinced me to stay." She smiled. "They really took good care of me. They transferred me to the warehouse—where I learned to drive a forklift and worked to load and unload the trucks—and they gave me a hefty raise."

"Most people would not have possessed the inner strength to return to work after such an ordeal," Susan said softly. "It's a token of your strength and determination."

"I don't feel strong," she admitted with a wry smile. "I'm actually scared to death right now. My biggest fear was that someone would come here and tell me Bud was back in town and he was coming for me. I hope that's not why you're here."

"No, I'm here to tell you he's dead," I said bluntly. "You'll never have to worry about him again."

Winona held her glass in midair. She opened her mouth to talk, but nothing came out. She worked her jaw for a bit and then asked in a squeaky voice. "He's dead?"

"Yes, ma'am."

She cleared her throat. "What happened? Where has he been? I mean, how do you know it's him? Are you sure?"

"Yeah, we're sure." I took out the driver's license and handed it to her. "This was taken off of his person and his medical records have all but proven it's him. He's been dead and buried for thirty years."

"Thirty years? You mean to tell me I've been living in fear all this time for no reason?" She shook her head incredulously, her chin trembling. "How did he die?"

"He was murdered," I said.

"Murdered?" she echoed. "But...but who murdered him?"

Leah leaned forward and touched Winona's trembling hand. "That's why we're here. We need to find his accomplice or accomplices, and we need your help."

Winona scowled. "My help? What can I do? I thought he was still on the run."

Leah reached for the file folder she had prepared and dug out the old canvass logs from thirty years past. She slid them to Winona. "I need you to study these names carefully. These people either lived in the canyon where the armored truck was dumped, or they were staying there at the time. We need to know if Bud ever mentioned any of these people or if you all ever met up with these people on your route. Maybe they worked at a pick up or drop off point? Maybe they frequented the video store? Anything at all might help."

"Bud was pretty quiet," Winona said idly as she began scanning the names. "He mostly talked about his daughter or some movie he watched. I tuned him out for the most part."

We all sat in silence as Winona put on her reading glasses and began scanning the lists of names. My phone buzzed in my pocket and I excused myself from the table.

While it was hot in the sun, it was surprisingly cool in the shade of the small porch, and this surprised me. In Louisiana, it didn't matter if you were in the direct sunlight or the shade—there was no escaping the smothering heat. Another thing I'd noticed was that my sinuses were dry. I didn't know if I liked that or not.

"This is Clint," I said without looking at the number.

"I found something." It was Amy. "Check your text messages. I'm sending it now."

I pulled the phone from my ear and checked the display screen. There was a close-up picture of two men walking out of Mitch Taylor's Corner Pub.

"Are these our guys?" I asked, putting the phone back to my ear.

"Yep. I spoke to the bartender and she remembered them being there when Joseph Billiot and the asshole from New Orleans got into it. She said they paid for their drinks with a hundred-dollar bill and gave her another one as a tip."

"Did she know their names or anything more about them?"

"The only thing she remembers them saying was that they

couldn't drink much because they had a long drive in front of them."

"Amy, you're the best!"

"If that were true, I'd have a husband or at least a boyfriend by now," she remarked dryly.

I didn't touch that one. Instead, I thanked her again and stepped back into the house. I had been seated at the table for another fifteen minutes or so when Winona shook her head and slid the lists of names back to Leah.

"I don't recognize any of these names."

"I have a picture I want you to look at," I said. "We captured our two suspects on video surveillance footage as they were leaving a barroom."

Winona lurched back in her chair and clutched at her throat. "Oh, God, are they coming for me?" She cast wild eyes from Leah to Susan to me and then back to Leah. "Is my life in danger?"

Leah moved closer and put a reassuring hand on her shoulder. "No, you're not in danger."

"How can you say that?" Winona demanded. "You don't have them in custody, so how can you say I'm not in danger? You think they killed Bud, so what's to stop them from coming for me?"

"We'll keep you safe—I promise."

The guarantee from Leah seemed to satisfy Winona and she took my phone in her trembling hands. Tears had welled up in her eyes and she had to reach under her reading glasses to brush them away. After peering at the image on my phone, she shook her head and handed it back to me.

"I don't recognize either of them."

I cursed under my breath. We had a description of a truck and a picture of our suspects, but they were almost useless without a name.

Leah's phone must've buzzed, because she glanced down at it and began reading something. When she bit down and began to shake her head, I knew it wasn't good.

"That son of a bitch!"

"What is it?" Susan and I asked in unison.

"My chief just texted me—a dentist from Windrift just held a press conference in front of his office and declared that he has positively identified the remains of Bud Walker." She shook her head. "Now the entire media is burning up the phone lines at the police department."

I pointed toward her phone. "Tell him to say nothing about this case! We need to keep this under wraps. Our suspects will haul ass if they know we're on to them."

"It might already be too late," she said, holding up her cell phone so I could see a news article stating that the remains of Bud Walker had been discovered somewhere in Louisiana.

I cursed again, but this time it was out loud.

CHAPTER 37

"Let's get back to that canyon," I told Leah when we were standing outside of Winona's home. "Someone out there has to know something."

"But Winona didn't recognize any of the names," Leah said. "Besides, most of the people who were living there thirty years ago are long gone."

I mulled over what she'd said. I glanced at Susan. "What do you think?"

"I think it's worth a shot," she said with a frown. "We don't have much else to go on, and it certainly wouldn't hurt to make a drive through there and knock on some doors."

Leah shifted her feet.

"What is it?" I asked.

"I need to get back to the office," she said. "I have to get the description of the truck and the pictures of the suspects out to my officers and to the surrounding counties. I also have to get it out to the highway patrol. In thirty years, this is the closest I've come to catching them and—now that the media's gotten ahold of it—I'm afraid they'll disappear again. If that happens, it's over. We'll never catch them."

"I can take Clint's Tahoe and deliver the information to your chief," Susan offered. "Clint can jump in with you and y'all can check out the canyon."

"Thank you!" Leah seemed relieved. She asked Susan for her cell number and then began typing something into her own phone. "I'm sending you my chief's contact information and the password to my computer. Upload a digital copy of the surveillance pictures on my computer and make a flyer with the description of the truck. Print out twenty copies and give them to the chief. He'll do the rest." She then turned to me. "Let's go!"

After grabbing my AR-15 for emergencies, I stepped onto the running board and settled into my seat. Leah wasted no time leaving Winona's neighborhood. She drove faster than I would've driven down the narrow streets, but I was far out of my jurisdiction and wasn't about to pass judgment.

"How many detectives do y'all have?" I asked.

"Two fulltime and two who are part time." She braked hard at a stop sign and then sped forward when she saw it was all clear. "Our population is small, but the town is spread out over sixty square miles of rugged terrain, so we need at least four for the coverage."

I nodded. While I was making idle talk, my mind was anything but idle. I was thinking ahead to what we might find in the canyon neighborhood. What if the suspects had already gotten wind of Bud's identification and had been spooked? I agreed with Leah's assessment that this was our last chance to catch these killers. They had gone thirty years without being caught. It spoke to tremendous discipline on their part. By now, most killers would've said something to someone, and whispers would've begun to leak out.

And how does someone bury two million in cash and just sit on it for thirty years? While it was difficult for most people to keep a secret, it would've been almost impossible for any normal person to leave that much money buried in the ground and not touch it. People dip into their savings or borrow against their 401(k)s every day for any number of perceived emergencies, such as college tuition, the once-in-a-lifetime family vacation, or ten percent down on a dream home. But to have that much money in the ground and never touch it for any reason—I had to admire these people.

"We're almost there," Leah said, turning onto a familiar road. When we drove past the juniper tree, I knew exactly where we were. She continued down a pathway that was narrow and winding. Most of the surface was loose rock and we left a cloud of dust in our wake. The suspects would be able to see us coming from miles away, thanks to the smoke signal we were sending up. I only hoped they wouldn't be able to recognize that it was a police vehicle until we were already upon them.

"Is there another way out of this canyon?" I asked.

"There is, but it's impassable," she explained, her voice breaking up with the violent jostling of the truck on the uneven surface. "We had a rockslide about two years ago that closed off the eastern pass.

The county doesn't have much money for infrastructure and there weren't enough travelers in that area to justify the expense, so they left it closed. They keep saying they'll get to it next year, but next year never seems to get here."

Leah turned abruptly to the right and the truck dipped suddenly as we left the rim of the canyon and began a deep descent into the valley below. The wall of rock to our left seemed to grow taller as we continued forward and it blocked the sun from our view. The valley was to our right and I could see a smattering of homes scattered across the canyon floor.

"Does this road go by every house in the canyon?" I asked.

"No. We have to go off road to reach a dozen of them." Leah tapped the file folder on the console between us. "The easiest places to access are the vacation homes, and we're hitting those last. If the killers are from here, they're locals and they live deep in the rocks."

I was inclined to agree with her, but I couldn't be sure. It wouldn't be easy to plan a heist from a vacation home, but it could explain how they were able to disappear for thirty years.

We left the road several times to check out different homesteads. Out of the five places we checked, four were occupied and one was empty. While nearly everyone had a 4x4 pickup, there wasn't one Silverado and not a single person matched the pictures of our suspects.

"There're two permanent places left to check before we make the rounds of the vacation homes," Leah said, her voice betraying her concern. It seemed to transfer to her right foot, because she began driving faster. "I hope this wasn't a waste of time."

I grunted inwardly. Considering it was my idea to be out there, I hoped it wasn't a waste of time either. I got a call from Susan saying she had given the information to the receptionist and she was now patrolling the town with the chief in search of the suspects. She said they had called out every officer on the force, including their auxiliary officers, and they were crawling all over the county.

"Oh, and the media found Winona Munday," she said before hanging up. "One of the local reporters remembered her being mentioned in the initial stories thirty years ago and they dug up her current address. They're reporting live from her front yard."

"Is she talking to them?"

"From what the chief said, she just went outside and told them to leave or she would call the police."

When we ended the call, I told Leah what Susan had said. She punched the steering wheel.

"Why can't those vultures just leave her alone?" she grumbled. "When she was in the ICU, several reporters camped outside the hospital waiting for her to be released. We had to sneak her through the back to get her home, but it didn't take them long to find her house. She had to move twice before the story grew old and they got bored with it. She's probably terrified."

I considered that. "She was your only witness. Without her, there would've been no case against Bud."

"Yep."

"Do you think she's a threat to the new suspects?"

"I don't see how. She didn't see anyone but Bud, so they were never on our radar." She shook her head. "In all of the years that followed, I never believed he had an accomplice. I figured if he did, someone would've talked by now."

I was about to open my mouth to speak when the road took a sharp turn to the left and the right shoulder suddenly disappeared into thin air. The road had narrowed considerably. We were now on a one-lane stretch with nowhere to go on the left and only a steep drop-off to the right. It was at least fifty feet to the bottom, and there wasn't a guardrail to keep us honest. I instinctively reached for the grab handle.

"I guess you don't have roads like this where you're from," Leah commented, glancing at me with a wry smile.

"Nah, the tallest mountain we have in Mechant Loup is this giant ant pile near the Bayou Tail Boat Launch." I relaxed when she slowed down a bit. I wasn't as worried about the drop-off as I was about her driving. She might be the best driver this side of the Mississippi, or she might be the worst. I just didn't know and I had a daughter and wife to get back to.

CHAPTER 38

After driving for a few minutes, the road curved back to the right and away from the canyon wall. We had almost reached the canyon floor and I started to relax. Law enforcement was an uncertain and risky profession filled with all kinds of dangerous pitfalls, but at least I knew I wouldn't be falling to my death just yet.

Leah drove for another mile or so and then slowed to a stop. I glanced curiously at her. Her face scrunched up. She shoved the gearshift in reverse and backed up for about a hundred feet.

"What is it?" I asked when she stopped and stared toward the distant wall of the canyon. It was at least a hundred yards away and the area between us was littered with sagebrush and an occasional juniper.

She pointed to a vertical shadow in the far-off rock. "You see that shaded area?"

I nodded.

"It's a crack in the rock. It looks small from here, but it's big enough to fit a truck." She pointed to a clump of nearby sagebrush and then to a thin wisp of dust in the distance. "That sage has been smashed recently and that dust is from someone driving through here."

"Is there a house back there?"

"Supposedly, but I've never seen it. I had missed it when we did the initial canvass thirty years ago, but my chief told me about it." She reached for her canvass logs and thumbed through them. "Here it is. No one was home at the time of the canvass and I couldn't access the property because of a large gate that blocked the driveway."

"You couldn't go around it?"

"There's a solid wall of rock on either side of the driveway and the gate is fastened to the rock. It's smooth and tall, so I wasn't able to scale it."

"Have you ever spoken to him?"

"I did a phone interview with him a week after the heist. According to my notes, he wasn't home at the time and didn't see or hear anything."

"Who is he?"

"Duke Smith is his name." She shrugged and handed me a faded printout. "I don't know much about him. I ran his rap sheet back then, but he was clean."

I read the information on the driver's license printout, but nothing stood out. "Are we checking in on him?"

"It's a rough ride to the gate." She hesitated, seemingly gauging the distance and the time it would take. "Let's go check out these last two houses first. Whoever drove through here won't be back before we're done. The terrain between here and there is too rough for getting out in a hurry."

So saying, she drove to the last two houses and we interviewed the last of the permanent residents. Neither of the families had lived in the area thirty years ago, so they were useless. None of them had even heard of the armored car heist, and they had more questions than we had time to answer.

We were about to leave the last house when Leah had a thought and stopped abruptly. She turned to the man and woman who stood on the porch of their log cabin.

"Do you guys know the man who lives in the crack back there?" she asked. "His name is Duke Smith."

The man and wife exchanged glances, and the man nodded. "Yeah, I've met him once or twice over the past six years," he said. "He doesn't talk much, but he always waves when he sees me."

"Yeah," the wife confirmed. "He seems to be nice. He waves when we pass him on the road. I've never said anything to him, but I see him once or twice per month on my way to town. I think he has some cows, because he's usually hauling hay from town."

"They do have a few head of cattle," the husband offered. "I've had half a dozen conversations with his son and he's mentioned the cattle. I think they also have a couple of horses, but they don't have much grass up there, so they have to haul it in."

"You've spoken with the son?"

"Yes, ma'am. We've talked about hunting before. He asked if I have any animals. He's spoken about their horses and cows." The husband was thoughtful. "Oh, yeah, and then he warned me about some rattlesnakes one time. My daughter and I were walking on a trail and we ran into him. He pointed out a couple of spots where he'd seen some big ones. He's always been nice and helpful."

"He gives me the creeps," the wife said, shuddering. "I roll my window up when I see him on the road."

The man chuckled. "She thinks everyone's creepy."

"Do you know what they drive?" Leah asked before the woman could object.

"When I see the old man, he's always on a tractor," the husband said. "Jimmy usually rides a four-wheeler or a dirt bike."

"Jimmy?" Leah asked.

"Yeah, that's the son's name."

Leah and I glanced at each other.

"If I showed you a picture of two men, would you be able to tell me if they were Duke and Jimmy?" Leah asked.

The man scowled and shifted the cowboy hat on his head. "I doubt it. It's bright out here and everyone wears hats and sunglasses. But if you want me to try, I'd be happy to do it."

Leah gave me a nod and I pulled out my phone. The man squinted to see the small image. He had to cup his hands around it to block out the glare of the sun. After a few minutes, he shook his head.

"I really can't be sure," he said. "The body styles and sizes are about right, but it's hard to say with any degree of certainty. What did they do?"

Leah waved a hand in the air. "It's nothing to be concerned about."

We thanked the couple and headed back in the direction from whence we'd come.

"What do you think?" I asked Leah.

"There're probably 300,000 people in the United States named Jimmy. Do you know how lucky we'd have to be for this to be the right one?" She shot me a sideways glance. "And I don't get lucky."

I nodded in agreement and held on as she turned the nose of her truck toward the north and headed straight for the far away wall. The road was so rough that my teeth rattled inside my head. She jerked to the left and right often to avoid juniper trees, but she plowed right through the sagebrush.

Small animals scurried from the brush as we approached. Some of them looked like squirrels, but they were different from the ones I was accustomed to seeing. I even saw a coyote break and run from where it was sitting in the shade of a juniper.

When we were about twenty yards from the crack in the rock, I caught sight of the gate. She was right. It was tall and ominous. It appeared to be constructed of solid steel. If the size of the hinges were any indication of the care that had gone into strengthening the gate, there would be no driving through the thing. Without the assistance of a man lift, I didn't know how we would be able to scale the fence.

"It looks locked," I said.

She nodded as she pulled up to the gate and shut off the engine. "We don't have a warrant to tear it down. Even if we did have a warrant, it would take a bulldozer to knock this thing down."

We dismounted and walked to the gate. Leah checked the lock and I checked the hinges. Both sides were impenetrable. Based on the positioning of the hinges, the gate swung outwardly. On the opposite end, the fence was married to the frame as though it had been welded in place. There was no place to attach a chain or rope.

I looked up. The gate was at least twelve feet high. Even if Leah stood on my shoulders, she wouldn't be able to see over the top. However, if I stood in the bed of her truck and she stood on my shoulders, then we might be able to see into the property.

"Do you think these are our guys?" I asked, looking to where Leah had dropped to the ground and was trying to see under the gate. She stood to her feet and cursed as she wiped the red dust off of her front.

"The gate melds into the footer like they were carved out of a single piece of steel." She shook her head and continued studying the gate. "I don't know why you would fortify your homestead if you weren't hiding something illegal on your property."

I nodded, lost in thought. I wanted a gate like that to secure our property. After the attack on the women's shelter Susan used to run, we had shut it down because it wasn't fortified enough to keep out the most determined criminals. But with a gate like this and a fence around the entire property, we would be able to adequately protect the women who needed our help the most.

"Clint!" Leah's voice snapped me out of my thoughts. "Did you hear me?"

I glanced at her and heard it before I could say anything. A vehicle was approaching the gate!

CHAPTER 39

Leah and I scrambled to her truck. She backed it away from the gate and angled it on the side with the hinges.

"As soon as the gate opens, I'm going through it," she said breathlessly. "I'll act confused, like I thought they were opening it for us, but I really want to box them in. If they're involved in the heist, I don't want them escaping again. It's taken too long to get this close, and I'll do whatever it takes to get them in custody."

I nodded. Lifting the tail of my shirt on my right side, I tucked it behind my pistol grip. I wanted easy access to it just in case things went south in a hurry.

Both of our windows were down and we could hear the tires rolling across the rocky road. The brakes squealed when the vehicle eased to a stop directly on the other side of the gate. Within seconds, there was a whining sound, a screech, and then the large gate lurched in place. After a momentary pause, it began to slowly swing open.

"Come on," Leah said under her breath. "Come to momma."

As soon as the gate was wide enough to squeeze through, Leah punched the accelerator. She drove around the gate and into the opening, which was only wide enough for one vehicle at a time. She stopped abruptly when we came face-to-face with a dark gray Silverado pickup truck. I locked eyes on the driver, who was directly across from me. We were separated by the length of two hoods, plus a few feet. In the cool shade of the canyon wall, I could plainly see through the front windshield and knew instantly he was the man from the surveillance video that Amy had recovered. I glanced at the passenger. He was definitely the younger guy.

"It's them," I said to Leah. "It's definitely them."

"Yep." She smiled and waved to the men, then reached for her door handle. "It's about to get real."

I followed suit and stepped out of her truck. I was trying to act relaxed, but I was anything but. My hand stayed close to my pistol and my eyes were focused like a laser on the driver.

"I've got the driver," I muttered. Duke's hands were on the steering wheel, right where I liked them.

"Stop right there!" the younger man said, sticking his head out of the window. "You're on private property and we don't consent to your presence."

Leah stopped walking and raised her hands. "We're here on official business."

"And I'm officially saying we don't give consent to any unlawful searches." His voice was level and confident. "If you don't have a warrant, I'm going to have to ask you to get back in your truck and remove it from blocking our egress."

"I just need to ask some questions about that armored car heist from thirty years ago," Leah said evenly.

I could tell she was pressing the issue. She wanted to force their hands. If they made a move, they were definitely our men. If they knew nothing about the heist, they would be confused and relieved that we weren't there for some other reason.

"What'd she say?" Duke asked Jimmy. He had taken his eyes off of me momentarily to turn and look at his son. When Jimmy told him what Leah had said, he turned back to face me and I could see his face was tense.

Duke leaned his head out of the window. I noticed that his right hand had slipped off of the steering wheel. "You have no authority on my land. You need to move your truck now!"

"I just need to know if you guys saw anything suspicious that night thirty years ago," Leah said in a conversational tone. "If you'd feel more comfortable, we can back out and have that conversation out in the opening—off of your land."

The two men exchanged words that we couldn't hear. Finally, Jimmy leaned out and agreed to her terms. "Back your truck out so we can drive clear of the gate," he said. "Once we're on public land and our gate is closed, we'll talk. We don't want our cows and horses to get loose."

Not taking our eyes off of them, Leah and I backed toward our doors and got in.

"Did you notice the mud on the side of the truck?" I asked.

"Yeah," she said as she settled into the driver's seat. "It looks weird. It's black or dark gray."

"That's Louisiana mud," I explained. "There's no red stuff in the swamps."

"No kidding?"

I nodded, and asked, "What do we know so far?"

Leah used her side mirrors to back out of the opening, so she could keep her head forward. "They were definitely in Louisiana during the time of that young boy's murder, the money they spent in your town was definitely from the time period of the heist, and they're definitely armed."

I agreed with everything she said. Trying not to move my shoulder much, I eased my pistol from the holster and rested it on my leg.

"What's our move?" I asked, never taking my eyes from Duke, who had begun to drive his truck forward.

"It depends on what they do." Leah had now backed her truck far enough for the tailgate of Duke's truck to clear the gate. "I'm hoping they want to talk, but my gut is telling me otherwise."

Leah shifted her truck in *park* and we sat waiting for them to come through the gate.

"What're they doing?" Leah asked when Duke stopped the truck in the middle of the opening, blocking it from ingress or egress. "Why'd he stop?"

I was about to open my mouth to shout a warning, but it was drowned out by gunfire.

Jimmy had suddenly leaned out of the truck and stuck an AK-47 in our direction and, without warning, had begun firing upon us. I grabbed Leah by the collar of her shirt and jerked her toward me. As bullets riddled the windshield and metal framework, I threw myself over her body and tried to push her deeper into the upholstery. Glass shards exploded violently into the air and sprayed my back like a shotgun blast of rock salt.

We were sitting ducks. If I didn't do something quickly, I knew Jimmy could advance on our position and kill us where we crouched. I shifted to my left shoulder—making sure to stay below the level of the dashboard—and lifted the pistol that was still in my hand. I knew there was a chance I might get my hand shot off, but I had to take the chance.

Pointing my pistol in the direction of the semi-automatic gunfire, I began firing as fast as I could pull the trigger. The shots exploded inside the confined space and my ears began ringing instantly.

Leah was moving beneath my body, trying to squeeze out from

under me and onto the floor. Once she managed to get free of me, she lifted her own handgun and sent sixteen bullets zipping in the direction of our attackers.

I was already empty and began feeding a fresh magazine into the magazine well when I paused. Everything was quiet.

"Did we get them?" Leah asked, breathless.

In the silence that followed, my magazine clicked loudly when I pushed it into place. I shifted to reach for the door handle. Piles of glass dumped from my back and spilled onto the floor, some of it raining down on Leah.

I muttered an apology as I pulled the handle and shoved the door open. Nothing happened. All I heard was the high-pitch ringing in my ears. I glanced down at Leah, who had a befuddled expression on her face.

"Do you think we got them?" she asked.

I shot up and glanced through the busted-out windshield. Through the gateway and about fifty yards behind the dark gray Silverado, I could see Duke and Jimmy running for all they were worth.

"It was a diversion!" I hollered, scrambling out of the truck and dropping to the ground. "They're getting away!"

CHAPTER 40

There was no room for Leah and me to squeeze between the truck and the side walls of the gate, so we were forced to go over the top. As for me, I hit the front bumper of the dark gray Silverado on a dead run. Planting my left foot on the bumper, I leapt into the air and my right boot left a large dent in the hood. I don't know what method Leah utilized, but she was right behind me as I scrambled over the top of the truck and dropped to the bed. In two strides, I was across the bed and leaping to the ground.

Ahead of us, the terrain was rugged and it rose precipitously. Jimmy, who was still carrying the AK-47, had disappeared around an outcropping of rocks to the right. Duke had veered left and was heading straight for a stucco-style house that stood amongst a network of fences and gates that secured a dozen or so horses and cows. I went after Jimmy.

My thighs screamed as I advanced up the steep slope and approached the rocks behind which Jimmy had disappeared. I stopped when I reached the outcropping of rocks. I wasn't sure if it was a subconscious tactical move or if my legs had simply quit working for a second, but they certainly burned from the exertion of the steep climb. Taking a haggard breath, I did a quick-peek around a large rock. Jimmy was still running. He twisted his head around to check my progress, and I could see he was trying to fit another large magazine into the rifle.

Knowing I had to reach him before he reloaded that weapon, I burst out from behind the rock and sprinted for all I was worth.

"Put down the rifle or I'll shoot!" I hollered. As though the exertion wasn't bad enough, the yelling had just about done me in. I found myself fighting for air and my chest burned. I began to wonder what was wrong with me. I'd never felt this way before. Was I having a heart attack? I'd never been winded so quickly and my breathing had never seemed so shallow.

I was closing in on Jimmy and he could feel it. He stopped trying to load the rifle and, instead, turned to face me, swinging it like a club. I was still twenty feet away, but he began swinging it back and forth, as though it would create a force field behind which he could hide. He was screaming like a madman, his eyes wide and his teeth bared. His long, receding hair was disheveled and gave him the appearance of a wild animal that was cornered.

I slowed to measure my approach and to try and catch some air. I knew I had to fight, and I wanted to do so with an adequate supply of oxygen. He had just taken a swing to his left. I waited until he'd reached the very end of the swing. That was when I made my move.

I closed the distance between us in a flash. He yelped as he realized I was upon him and he was helpless. Since both of his hands were attached to the rifle, he couldn't block the punch I leveled at his chin. He was a heavy man and he went down hard. To my surprise, I went down with him. My best guess was that I had expected him to stay upright and had overextended my reach, which caused my right foot to slip out from under me on the smooth rock. My momentum did the rest.

I hit the ground on a forward motion, landing on top of Jimmy, but sliding forward. He helped me along be giving me a shove, and I suddenly found myself suspended in the air. I began to wonder at the strength of this man and how on earth had it been possible for him to fling me into space, but I then realized I had fallen over the cliff. At that same moment, I heard gunshots in the distance.

Confused, I clawed at the empty space around me like a wild cat fighting for its life. I saw the sky in one moment and then golden rocks in the next. Somehow—in what was either a fortuitous event or divine intervention—my right hand brushed against something round and rough. I clamped down as hard as I could. The rest of my body continued falling, but pulled up short when my arm reached its full extension. Thankfully, my grip held.

My shoulder ached, for it had been wrenched violently when my arm went taut, but I was relieved to be alive. I did what one should never do in such a position—I looked down. My head spun and I instantly became nauseous. Seventy feet below me was a dry river bed filled with large boulders and hard-packed earth. If I fell, there would be no surviving the drop.

I slowly lifted my head—still trying to catch my breath—and saw Jimmy standing on the ledge above me, a wicked grin playing across his lips. I also saw a small juniper tree growing out of the side of the rock. I had grabbed one of the branches. While it had felt sturdy when it broke my fall, it sure didn't look like much.

"What's the matter, boy?" Jimmy's tone was mocking. He was calmly reloading the AK-47 as he spoke. "Can't breathe? You see, the air's thinner up here in the mountains. You've got to learn to do more with less. When I was down in Louisiana, I felt like I was inhaling pure oxygen. It made me high. It was like a natural drug."

"Why'd you do it?" I asked, trying to stall for time and search for a way out of this dire situation.

"For the money, of course."

"No, why kill the boy?"

"Oh, that." The magazine locked into place and Jimmy allowed the rifle to dangle in his right hand, the muzzle aiming in my direction. "We were almost home free when that little shit came snooping around. I knew if we left him alone he would direct the authorities to Bud, and I knew if we killed him the authorities would be crawling all over that area and probably find the grave. It was a no-win situation, and you have to make the best of what you've got, you know? We hung around town for an extra day to see if it had caused a stir, but there are too many hotheads in your little shit town. Sooner or later, I would've dropped one of those Cajun assholes and we would've gotten picked up. That would not have been good for our plans."

I was still breathless and my right hand was aching. I couldn't hold on forever. I was eventually going to slip. Moving my feet very slowly—careful not to put undue strain on my grip—I felt for a foothold in the rock.

"Did you kill Bud?" I asked, still exploring the wall with my foot.

"It doesn't matter who killed Bud," he said dryly.

I finally felt a tiny opening in the rock. I applied pressure with the toe of my right boot and it held. Relieved, I glanced back up at Jimmy. He had closed his left eye and was focused on the front sight of the rifle with his right eye. I couldn't be positive, but it looked like he was aiming directly at my forehead.

"Why'd y'all wait so long to retrieve the money?" I asked in a conversational tone, trying to keep him talking.

"Retirement," he said absently.

"Retirement?"

"Yeah, the normal retirement period is thirty years." He shifted the muzzle of the rifle from my head to my right hand, as though trying to decide if he wanted me to die instantly or fall to my death. "Had we begun spending the money right away, we would've attracted too much attention. Had we stashed it on our ranch, someone would've found it. But after thirty years, no one would've remembered that old heist—that is, until you came along and screwed up our retirement. For that, you'll have to die."

"Had you not killed Zeke McKenzie, you'd be enjoying your retirement right now." Putting most of my body's weight on my right foot, I adjusted my grip on the tree branch. "Look, I think we can work something out. If you kill me, you'll certainly get the firing squad—isn't that still an option here in Utah?"

"That's how real men decide to go out." He grinned wickedly again. "Are you a real man? Do you want to fall to your death like a little bitch or be shot like a man? Pick your poison, son. You're getting the death sentence, and you get to decide how you're leaving this earth. As for me, I'll be long gone before they even find you and your partner. You heard those gunshots, didn't you? Yeah, you did. That was my dad taking out your partner. It's over for you, boy."

As I stared up into his gray eyes, I knew I was looking into the eyes of an animal. Even if this man didn't need to kill Zeke, he probably would've done it for fun. There was no talking him out of killing me and there was no stopping him. I had lost my pistol when I'd grabbed for the branch and, while I'd prefer to go down fighting, I couldn't even reach him.

"Or you can beg for your life like a little bitch." Jimmy chuckled. "What's it going to be?"

"You can go to hell, Jimmy," I said, holding my head upright, ready to accept my fate. "You're a coward and a loser. You'll never amount to shit."

Jimmy snarled and pulled the trigger.

CHAPTER 41

When Clint Wolf had turned to pursue Jimmy Smith, Leah had broken away and made a beeline for Duke. The elderly man could run fast for his age, but he was no match for Leah. She closed the distance within a minute.

"Duke Smith, you're under arrest!" Leah shouted as she came to within twenty yards of the heavy man. "Stop running and get your ass on the ground!"

As though he could feel her bearing down on him, Duke reached toward his belly with his right hand and whipped around in midstride. Detecting the subtle movement of Duke's right hand, Leah dove to the ground—dipping her shoulder as she did so—and fell into a tactical roll just as Duke began blasting shots from a semi-automatic pistol.

When Leah came out of her roll, her pistol was up and she returned fire. While all of Duke's bullets ricocheted harmlessly off the orange rocks to Leah's left, four of her seven shots found their mark. Duke's T-shirt was white and the red blotches that appeared when he was struck by the bullets provided instant feedback.

Two of the bullets struck Duke in the lower abdomen, but they didn't slow him down. Seeing the red blotches low on his torso, Leah raised her aim slightly and her next two rounds struck her attacker higher—one in his neck and the other in his chest. Duke stumbled forward, but managed to regain his balance and keep from falling. He opened his mouth to voice an objection, but he was unable to utter an intelligible word. He clamped his mouth shut and tried to lift his gun hand, but was unable to do so.

"Drop the gun!" Leah said, rising slowly to her feet and keeping her pistol trained on the man.

Duke clutched at the holes in his chest with his left hand, as though trying to stop the blood from flowing. Finally, with a befuddled look on his face, he sat down hard on the ground and slumped over.

Leah moved in quickly and kicked the pistol away from Duke's outstretched hand. Seeing he was no longer a threat, she holstered her weapon and gently rolled Duke onto his back to assess his condition. He was definitely gut shot and would die without medical assistance. The wound to the right side of his neck apparently clipped a nerve, because his right hand hung limp at his side. The chest wound most certainly missed his heart, but it had probably penetrated the upper portion of his lung.

Leah snatched her portable radio from her belt and, after giving her location and announcing that shots had been fired and one suspect was down, she requested immediate medical assistance. Even as she made the request, she knew there was no way the medics would arrive in time to save the man.

Although Duke had just tried to murder her, she tried to make him more comfortable. She ripped the sleeve off of her shirt and pressed it to the wound in Duke's neck, because it was bleeding more freely than the others.

"Mr. Smith, I'm not going to lie to you, it's bad," she said in a solemn, but kind, voice. "You're dying."

He let out a grunt, but nodded. "I…I know. I can feel…can feel it."

"Do you believe in Heaven and hell?"

He nodded again.

"Well, if you want to make it into Heaven, you need to confess your sins." Leah leaned closer to his face. "I need you to tell me who killed the young boy in Louisiana."

Duke shook his head and closed his eyes.

"His name was Zeke McKenzie," Leah said more forcefully, "and he was fourteen years old. His family deserves to know who did this to him."

Duke opened his eyes and Leah was sure she saw tears leaking down his face.

"Please," she said, "help me give the family some closure."

"Jimmy," Duke said in a hoarse and weak voice. "Jimmy hit him…hit him…um, with a shovel."

"Did he catch you guys digging up the money?"

Duke closed his eyes and gave a half nod.

"Who killed Bud Walker?"

Duke opened his mouth to speak, but a sudden gasp ripped from his throat. Blood gurgled from his throat. His eyes widened. He reached for Leah's face with his left hand, but she pushed it away. He lay there struggling for air, clutching wildly with his left hand. Fear filled his eyes.

"Hang on, Mr. Smith, help is on the way," Leah said soothingly, knowing it was a lost cause. She didn't bother asking another question, because he was already gone.

Leah quickly stood and glanced toward where she'd last seen Clint Wolf. A frown played across her mouth as she realized that her interaction with Duke Smith had taken several minutes. Clint should've been back by now with Jimmy in handcuffs. She was relieved to not have heard the report of that AK-47 again, but she was troubled that Clint had not reappeared.

As she sprinted in the direction of the rugged terrain where Clint and Jimmy had disappeared, she hit the magazine release button on her pistol and quickly replaced it with a fresh and fully loaded magazine. She ran up a steep slope and headed for an outcropping of rocks. Once she rounded the corner, she found herself in a stretch of rugged territory. She stopped briefly and surveyed the area. Thinking quickly, she figured there was only one route Jimmy could have taken, and she headed in that direction.

She had run about a hundred yards when she rounded another corner and came upon a scene that terrified her. Still running forward at a full sprint, she immediately interpreted what she was seeing.

Jimmy Smith was standing at the edge of a cliff, and he was aiming his AK-47 at Clint Wolf, who was out of sight over that cliff and somewhere below Jimmy. She also knew there was no way she could get off an accurate and lifesaving shot on a dead run, so she did the only thing she could do—she closed the distance in several bounding steps. Without uttering even a whisper of a warning, she jumped into the air and kicked Jimmy right in the back with both of her feet. Simultaneous with him pulling the trigger, the heels of her boots crashed violently into his back and bent him in half in the wrong direction.

Leah fell to the ground with a thud just as Jimmy disappeared over the edge of the cliff. Without wasting any time, she scrambled to her hands and knees and crawled rapidly to the cliff's edge, calling out Clint's name.

CHAPTER 42

Just as Jimmy pulled the trigger, I kicked off with my right foot and lunged to the left, trying desperately to maintain my grip on the juniper tree. My body swung wildly in that direction. I kept my eyes fixed upward, but stared dumbfounded as Jimmy did a violent pelvic thrust right over the edge of the cliff. The AK-47 flung from his hands and he screamed all the way to the canyon floor.

As I swung back toward my right, I explored wildly with my right foot until I reclaimed the foothold. After checking to make sure the rugged rocks below had served up justice, I glanced up to see what had caused him to plunge to his death.

"Clint!"

I heard Leah's voice a split second before I saw her face appear over the ledge. When she saw me, she sighed audibly.

"Thank God you're alive." She shook her head. "I have a feeling your wife would've killed me if anything bad would've happened to you."

Forgetting my plight for a moment, I asked what gave her that idea. I hadn't heard Susan say anything protective or threatening.

"It's just the way she looked at me when we left the station," Leah said. "I could tell she's very particular about your backup."

I laughed and then asked if she had any ideas. "I'm afraid this tree will break loose if I try to pull myself up to the ledge."

"It will," she said as she examined the trunk of the tree. "Don't move. It's barely hanging on as it is." She scrambled quickly to her feet. "Duke's truck has a winch on the front bumper. Just stay put for a few minutes."

"I'm not going anywhere," I hollered after her disappearing

figure. I glanced down again and gulped. If the tree broke loose, I'd be joining Jimmy, who had entered the afterlife in a splattered mess. I put more of my weight on my right foot and hugged the rock wall, praying that Leah would be back soon.

The heat from the rock wall burned my face. Sweat poured from my forehead and burned my eyes. I tried to blink them away, but it was no use. I dared not reach up and wipe my eyes. As I stood there clinging to life, I couldn't help but smile wryly when I realized I was the very definition of a cliffhanger at that moment.

I didn't have to wait long to hear the rumbling of the old Silverado. Thanks to the large boulders that littered the ground above me, Leah would not be able to get the truck close to the edge, but it turned out not to matter. The winch cable was long enough to reach me, and she was soon standing at the edge of the cliff.

"I'll drop this down to you," she said, holding up the end of the cable, which she'd fashioned into a loop. "As soon as you're situated, I'll have to go back to the truck to retract the cable."

I reached for the cable with my left hand and pulled it as far as it would go. I had to lift my left foot high, but managed to fit it into the loop. Saying a silent prayer, I flexed the muscles in my leg and pulled on the juniper branch, slowly lifting myself. I was almost upright when the juniper branch suddenly snapped.

Leah screamed as I fell. My left hand nearly caught fire as it slid rapidly down the cable. I squeezed for all I was worth, but it didn't even slow my descent. When my hand broke free from the cable, my body unfolded violently. My heart nearly leapt to my throat as I slammed against the rock wall. Miraculously, my foot had snagged in the loop and I was left hanging upside down, a mere seventy feet separating me from certain death.

"Oh, my God, Clint, are you okay?"

"Just pull me up," I whispered, afraid to breathe. "Just pull me up."

I heard her boots clattering against the rock as she rushed back to the truck. Within seconds, the cable jerked. I gasped out loud.

"Shit!" I took a calming breath. I was not ready to die, and I certainly didn't want to go out like this. I stole a glance at my boot as the cable began to pull me toward the rim. The loop had tightened around my boot and was strangling my ankle. It hurt, but I didn't care. I just didn't want it to let go.

Leah had fed the cable over a large boulder near the rim and it allowed the cable to lift me above the edge of the cliff. As soon as my head was clear of the edge, I clutched at the boulder and pulled my body away from the drop-off.

"Lower the cable!" I hollered. "I'm clear."

The cable lurched to a stop, and then reversed course. As it started to lower me, I clawed my way farther away from the edge. Once my entire body was safely resting on the rugged ground, I dragged my body several more feet from the edge and turned onto my back, exhausted and completely spent.

I don't know how long I lay there with my eyes closed, trying to calm my racing heart, but when I opened them, Leah and several other officers were standing there looking down at me. From somewhere in the distance, I heard Susan's voice demanding to know what was going on. That lit a fire under my ass.

I quickly pulled myself to my feet. "Thank you, Leah," I said. "You saved my life."

"Then we're even," she said.

I knew what she meant, and only nodded.

Susan approached us with the chief of police, a wiry man who wore a uniform too large for his frame. He looked like a teenager who had borrowed his father's clothes for prom.

Susan didn't ask any questions. There would be time for that later.

The chief walked to the edge of the cliff and looked down. "That's a good place for Jimmy Smith," he muttered. "He was never worth a shit."

"You knew him?" I asked.

"I went to school with him." He spat over the cliff. "He was voted most likely to end up in prison."

"He confessed to killing Zeke McKenzie," I offered.

"I'm not surprised," said the chief.

"His dad verified it," Leah said. "He was about to finger his son for killing Bud Walker when he died."

I told them what Jimmy had said about the heist, and the chief nodded his approval. He indicated Leah with a shake of the head and tossed her his keys.

"Take my truck and our friends from Louisiana and go to Winona Munday's house in a hurry. Media vans are crawling all over her neighborhood and she can't leave her house. Get her to the office so we can do a victim's notification in person and in private. See if she can help us connect these assholes to Bud Walker. Also, contact the armored car company and let them know we solved the case." He shot a thumb toward where Jimmy had been kicked off the cliff. "We'll clean up this mess and then search the Smith property for the stolen money."

CHAPTER 43

The tires on Leah's truck screeched when she braked hard in front of Winona Munday's house an hour later. There were four news vans parked along the sidewalk that lined the street and one of them was blocking Winona's driveway. Reporters and cameramen were crowding the tiny garden. Some were even tromping the flowers.

"Get the hell out of her yard!" Leah commanded, jumping from her truck like she was ready to fight a grizzly bear.

I dropped down on my side of the truck and my right knee buckled. I didn't know if my legs were fatigued from the rough uphill run earlier or if I was still shaken from nearly falling to my death. Either way, Susan noticed and cast a concerned look in my direction. I waved her off. She didn't say anything.

Although we were over a thousand miles outside of our jurisdiction, we joined Leah in pushing back the media.

"And move this damn van right now or I'll have it towed!" Leah spat the words, glaring around in search of the driver of the news van that was blocking Winona's driveway.

A meek-looking cameraman rushed over, threw his equipment through the downed window, and then rushed inside to move the van. Once he had moved, Leah backed her truck in the driveway and then Susan and I followed her into Winona's house. Winona threw her hands around Leah's neck.

"Thank you so much! They're like vultures waiting to feed on a dead carcass." She released Leah's neck and pushed the curtain back to survey the front yard. "They've been here for over an hour. I don't even know how they found my address."

"We'll get you out of here," Leah assured the trembling woman. "I've got some news to share, but I want to do it down at the police station."

"Good news or bad news?"

Leah smiled. "Great news."

Winona's eyes lit up and she scurried around the living room gathering up her purse, shoes, and cell phone. Once she had the items in hand, she nodded.

"I'm ready."

The sun was going down when we headed outside, but it was much later than I thought it was, thanks to us being so far west and in a different time zone. Susan and I sat in the back so Winona could sit in the front seat with Leah. Susan leaned over to whisper in my ear.

"There's no way we're heading home tonight."

I nodded and reached for my phone with my left hand. When the palm of my hand brushed against my jeans, I winced. The flesh was torn from sliding down the cable, so I carefully used my fingers to retrieve the phone. I texted Amy to let her know we'd be another day or two, and Susan got on her phone to notify Melvin and my mom.

When we reached the end of Winona's street, Winona glanced in the side mirror and groaned. "They're following us!"

"Not for long," Leah said with a smirk. She stopped at the stop sign and snatched up her radio. "Ready, boys?"

The radio scratched to life and a chorus of 10-4s called back. She then abruptly turned left at the corner and sped off down the street. The speed limit was 25, but she was going at least 50. I glanced back and saw that the news vans were trying to keep up. Before we reached the end of the street, we met two patrol cars heading in the opposite direction. As soon as they passed Leah's truck, they closed the roadway behind us, cutting off their progress. From some distance behind the news vans, I could see more patrol cars approaching from the rear, boxing them in.

"What'll happen to them?" Winona asked.

"They'll get cited for speeding." Leah grinned. "And speeding fines are doubled in a residential neighborhood."

Before long, we arrived at the police department and Leah led us down a narrow hall and into an interview room. After asking Winona to sit in the room for a while, Leah returned to her desk and began running criminal history checks and gathering up as much information as she could from her desk. While she did that, Susan accessed a first aid kit that hung from the wall in the hallway and doctored up my hand.

After a few long minutes, Leah mentioned that it was taking too long to run all the necessary checks. She asked one of the officers in the squad room to continue cross-referencing names and addresses of all the players, and she gave Susan and me a nod.

"I've got enough here to brief Winona." She then led Susan and me back down the hallway. The interview room in the Windrift Police Department was about half the size of the interview room in our police station. Susan and Leah sat on one side of the small table in the room and Winona sat across from them. I stood near the door.

With a solemn expression on her face, Leah leaned forward and said, "It's finally over, Winona. As you already know, Bud Walker has been confirmed dead."

Winona nodded, but she was far from relaxed just yet. She knew there was more news to come, and she didn't seem to know if it would be good or bad.

"We've been able to identify the two men who unearthed Bud's remains to retrieve the money from the heist. They're also the ones who murdered the young boy in Louisiana." Leah removed two driver's license pictures and slid them toward Leah. "This is Duke Smith and his son, Jimmy. We're not sure if they played a role in the heist or not, but we're looking into that now."

"They couldn't have played a role in the heist," Winona said. "I mean, I didn't see them in the video store or in the parking lot, so I don't know how they could be involved. They must've met up with Bud later."

"That's the other angle we're pursuing," Leah said. "Either they were in on it or they came upon him later. Regardless, we believe they're the ones who killed Bud and buried him and the money in that grave."

Winona's face was blank as she studied the photographs. "Aren't these the same men in the pictures from earlier? The pictures on his"—she pointed toward me—"cell phone?"

Leah nodded her head. "We were hoping you might be able to shed some light on the connection between them and Bud. Do these names or faces ring a bell to you? Had you ever seen Bud interacting with them?"

"No, not at all."

"Have you ever seen them around the warehouse?"

"Not that I can remember." Winona shook her head for emphasis. "Were they there? Did they work with me? I don't remember them ever being around, but it's a large company."

"We're not really sure. At this point, anything's a possibility and nothing's certain." Leah leaned back in her chair and folded her arms in front of her breasts. "I've cross-referenced Bud's name with their names and nothing comes back."

"Do they have the money from the heist?" Winona asked.

"We believe so. We've got people searching their property now." Leah looked at me and shook her head. I could tell she was frustrated. "Hopefully they'll find a taped confession along with the money—otherwise we may never know the truth."

"Why don't you ask this Duke and that Jimmy what happened?" Winona offered. "Couldn't they tell you who killed Bud and what they did with the money?"

"They can't," Leah said simply.

Winona cocked her head to the side. "Can't—or won't?"

"Can't. They're both dead."

Winona gasped and threw a hand to her mouth. "Dead? But how?"

"One took a dive over a cliff and the other took four bullets to the body." Leah stabbed at the driver's licenses on the table and set her jaw. "And this I can guarantee you—you will never have to worry about Bud or these men ever again."

"Are you saying it's finally over?" Winona asked through a stream of tears that began rolling down her face. "After all these years, can I finally start sleeping in peace again?"

Leah nodded. "Yes, you can."

"Will the nightmares go away?"

Susan grabbed a box of tissues that was on her side of the table and handed it to Winona. The woman took the tissues and muttered her thanks. As she dabbed at her eyes with a tissue, she asked a dozen questions about the case. She also asked me about Zeke and offered her condolences to his family.

"Had I only been stronger," she said tearfully, "had I pulled out my gun and stopped him, that young man wouldn't have had to die."

Leah immediately jumped in and told her that it was in no way her fault, and that the mere fact that she survived the beating was a testament to her strength.

"So…what do I do now?" Winona asked tentatively.

Leah smiled warmly. "You go home and live your life."

"But the media…"

"We can put you up in a hotel for a few days if you like," Leah offered. "It'll give the story time to die off. I'll pay for the room myself."

"No, I don't want—" Winona began, but was shushed by Leah.

"Nonsense, we'll drive by your house so you can pack an overnight bag. I'll make the arrangements."

As I stood there watching the back and forth, I felt my cell phone vibrate in my pocket. Excusing myself, I stepped into the hallway and answered.

"Hey, Clint," Amy began, "I know it's late where you are, but Karla said she got an urgent call from Albert Boudreaux. He said he needed you to call him back right away. Karla asked if it could wait until morning, but he said he needed to talk to you pronto."

"Do you have his number handy?" I asked. "I don't have my notes with me."

She gave me the number and I thanked her. Leah and Winona had stepped out of the interview room at that point and paused briefly so Winona could shake my hand.

"Thank you for your hard work," she said. "I'll be able to sleep in peace now, thanks to you."

I didn't like compliments, so I only nodded and wished her luck with her retirement. She said she would begin by sleeping for a week. We all laughed and Leah said she would meet Susan and me back at the police department once Winona was situated in a hotel room.

Susan stepped out of the interview room and shook her head as she watched them walk away. "We are such a long way from our retirement."

"Thank God," was all I said as I punched in Albert's number. I loved law enforcement work almost as much as I loved my family, and I dreaded the day when I'd be forced to walk away from my job.

Before I'd finished entering the number, my phone made a weird noise and I stared from the device to Susan. "What the hell is that sound?"

"It's FaceTime, you dinosaur!"

I grunted. I'd heard the ring on Susan's phone before, but never on mine. "What do I do now?"

"Give me that." Susan snatched the phone from my hand and fiddled with it. "It's Gracie and your mom!"

CHAPTER 44

Susan and I spent about ten minutes talking back and forth to Grace, who was still fired up after spending twelve hours in the Magic Kingdom. My mom looked ragged, but she was smiling nonetheless. I finally told them I had to make an important phone call and blew kisses at Grace.

"Detective Wolf?" Albert uttered excitedly when he answered my phone call. "I…I know the connection!"

"The connection? What connection?"

"I know how they knew about my family's land." He paused briefly to swallow. "Okay, so after talking to you the other day, I began to try and figure out what the connection was between my family and the body you found in the grave. It didn't make any sense. And then I saw earlier today that the man was identified as…as, um, Bud somebody or other?"

"Yeah, Bud Walker," I said, breaking through his excited utterance.

"Right, that was the name. It didn't mean anything to me at first, but then they said he was from Utah."

"That's correct," I said, standing a little straighter and listening more intently. "Did *that* mean something to you?"

"Well, I thought it was odd that the heist happened thirty years ago in Utah and the man who committed it was found buried in my back yard."

Although he couldn't see me, I shrugged. "I mean, he had to be buried somewhere. Other than him being so far from his home, why did you think it was odd?"

"Because I was actually living in Utah when the heist happened."

"You were?"

Susan detected the surprise in my voice, because her brow furrowed and she began hanging on my every word.

"Yes, sir," Albert said. "I was single at the time of the heist, but I had dated this girl from Utah a year earlier. It was before I'd met my wife. I actually brought her home to meet my parents two or three times. Each time I brought her home, I took her into the woods and we would hike all the way to our private lake. I'm not exactly sure where you found the grave, but if it was along this trail close to the lake, then I definitely brought her to that area."

I nodded, pondering what I was hearing and trying to guess where he was going with the information. When I didn't say anything, he continued.

"At first, I thought it was a strange coincidence, but then my wife just told me that two suspects were killed during an arrest in Windrift today."

I shook my head when he mentioned knowing about the officer-involved fatalities, remarking to myself how similar Mechant Loup was to Windrift when it came to keeping secrets.

"They mentioned the names of the two men and showed their pictures," Albert continued, "and I recognized them."

"You did?"

"Yes, sir. Jimmy's my ex-girlfriend's brother and Duke is her dad. And when I saw her on the news, I knew for sure that she was involved with the heist and she was the one who buried—"

"Wait—what?" I blurted, interrupting him. "You saw *who* on the news?"

"My ex-girlfriend from Utah—the one I brought to the woods behind my house," he explained. "It was her dad and brother who got killed during that arrest today. I saw her on the news and they were saying she was the victim in that armored car heist, but Winona had to be involved because she was the only one who knew about my property and—"

"Leah!" I hollered, dropping my phone from my ear and sprinting down the hallway. I reached the end and burst through the door and into the lobby. Without realizing it, I had pushed with too much force, causing the door to slam violently into the opposite wall. As I hit the exit door, I heard someone hollering from an office behind us, demanding to know what was going on.

I rushed into the parking lot and glanced around. We were too late. The chief's truck was long gone. Other than a couple of patrol trucks and my Tahoe, the lot was empty. I hurried back into the lobby and leaned against the receptionist's window.

"Can you get Leah on the radio right away?"

"Sure." She turned to a base station and called out Leah's radio number. I tapped my foot, but stopped abruptly when only static came back. "She didn't answer, so—"

"Where's the chief?" I asked impatiently.

"Um, they're all still out at the Smith property searching for the money," she said, staring down at her logbook. She mumbled to herself as she slid her finger down the page. "They requested a bulldozer and an excavator about two hours ago. They believe the money is hidden under the barn. I think they're going to tear the whole thing down. Um, let's see, they also ordered pizza thirty minutes ago—"

"Look, I need you to get a message to the chief right away," I said, already heading for the door. "Tell him Winona Munday's involved in the heist and she's got Leah."

"Huh?" the receptionist asked, looking up.

"Leah's in trouble!" I hollered. "Get some officers out to Winona Munday's house now!"

"What's going on?" Susan asked as she rushed after me and climbed into my Tahoe with me.

After asking her to hand me the Springfield 1911 in the glove box, I told her what Albert had said and what I suspected. I then asked her if she had noticed the freshly planted flowers in Winona's garden. She nodded slowly, thoughtfully.

"The money's in her garden," I said with certainty. "She's going for that money and then she's leaving town. God help Leah if she doesn't realize what's going on."

CHAPTER 45

Winona didn't speak much on the drive to her house, and Leah didn't press the issue. She knew it was an emotional time for her victim and she didn't want to contribute to her stress.

When Leah turned the chief's truck into Winona's driveway, the headlights illuminated the small garden out front. She frowned. "Those damn reporters trampled your flowers," she said, pointing to the damage.

"And I worked so hard on those flowers." Winona sighed and stepped out of the truck. She paused in the doorway and carefully surveyed the dark neighborhood. "You know, I'll be fine now. The reporters are gone and I don't think they're coming back. You scared them away."

Leah stepped out and met Winona in the front of the truck. "Are you sure? I can have you in a room within the hour. You can stay there as long as you like."

"I'd really like to see my daughters." Winona shifted her feet. "I think I'll pack my stuff and leave tonight. I'm serious, I'll be fine."

"I'll stand guard while you pack," Leah offered.

"Really, Detective Anderson, that's not necessary. You've done enough."

Leah smiled. "I insist."

Winona nodded and hurried into her house to gather up her things. Leah turned away and strode toward the driver's door. She glanced at the garden as she walked and stopped suddenly, something catching her eye. A clump of daylilies was resting on its side near a stepping stone. The flowers were beautiful and colorful. She moved closer and picked up the clump.

Leah then approached the small hole in the garden where the flowers had previously been planted. She squatted in that spot and scooped out a handful of dirt to make room for replanting the daylilies. When she did so, her fingers scraped against something solid but smooth a few inches into the soft topsoil.

"What the hell?" She scooped up several more handfuls of dirt and tossed them aside. A leather satchel slowly came into view. Curiosity getting the best of her, she pulled the satchel from the hole and unsnapped it. She gasped out loud when the glow from the truck's headlights revealed a bag filled with one-hundred-dollar bills wrapped in stacks of $10,000.

Suddenly, there was a subtle, yet distinct, metallic clicking noise behind her. She whirled around to see Winona standing there holding a silver revolver, and it was aimed directly at her.

"God, I wish you hadn't done that," Winona said sadly. "Of all the people in my life, you have been the most caring."

"What's going on?" Leah asked. She was confused. "Is this money from the heist?"

"Come on, Detective Anderson, you're not that stupid."

Leah's surroundings seemed to spin around like she was trapped inside a glass top. This couldn't be happening. This couldn't be right. "Are you saying you're involved in the heist?"

"Not *involved*," Winona corrected. "I helped to plan it."

"That can't be right." Leah almost forgot about the revolver aimed directly at her as she squatted in Winona's garden. "Bud beat the shit out of you and left you for dead. He almost succeeded in killing you."

"That wasn't Bud. It was Jimmy."

"Jimmy beat you up? But why didn't you tell me that? I would've arrested him."

"I couldn't." Winona sighed. "Jimmy's my brother and Duke's my dad."

Leah's mouth dropped open. Before she could respond, the radio in her chief's truck scratched to life and the dispatcher called out her call sign. She glanced longingly toward the truck.

"Don't even think about it," Winona said. "I won't hesitate to shoot you right there in my garden."

CHAPTER 46

After a long silence between them, Leah indicated Winona with a nod of her head. "I thought you told me your dad abused you and you ran away from home. You left Virginia to come here to get away from your dad—that's what you said in your statement. You begged me not to contact your family for fear that he would find you and abuse you again."

"It's what I had to say to get you on my side. I left my controlling mom and came here to Utah, where my real dad and brother were living." Winona frowned sadly. "I guess I've got no one now, thanks to you and those cops from Louisiana. Of course, it wouldn't have been long before you figured it out. Dad said Jimmy has been handing out hundreds like it was candy. He's crazy, you know. He killed that boy in Louisiana for no reason. And he...he wasn't supposed to hurt the clerk at the video store."

Leah's heart almost stopped beating at the shocking revelation about the clerk, but she said nothing. As long as Winona was willing to talk, she was willing to listen.

"If only he had listened," Winona said, shaking her head. "Jimmy was supposed to walk into the video store wearing a mask, tie up the girl, and lock her in the bathroom. When Bud walked in, Jimmy would get the drop on him, and Dad would walk in behind him to cut off his escape. They were supposed to tie him up and take his keys, but Jimmy screwed everything up when he deviated from the plan."

When Winona quit talking, Leah ventured softly, "What did Jimmy do to screw up the plan?"

"When Jimmy was alone with the girl, he...he attacked her and began violating her." Winona squeezed her eyes shut as tears began to flow. She lifted the revolver and scrubbed at her eyes with the back of her gun hand. Through the tears, she continued talking. "Dad heard her screaming from outside and went to investigate. He found Jimmy on top of her. Before he could intervene, Jimmy had choked her unconscious."

Although Winona was no longer pointing her gun at Leah, Leah didn't even think to go for her own gun. "Did Jimmy beat you as part of the plan to throw us off?"

Winona took a deep breath and exhaled. Nodding, she said, "And I think he took great pleasure in doing it. They were supposed to rough me up a little and leave me behind to make it look like Bud was part of the operation, but Jimmy got carried away. He really hurt me. If Dad hadn't pulled him off of me, I think he would've killed me."

"Did Bud see what Jimmy did to you?"

"No, he was already dead."

"Jimmy did it?"

"No—I did."

Leah stifled a gasp of shock. She didn't want to come across as judgmental. "You?"

"Yeah. When Bud went inside the video store, he saw Dad and Jimmy standing over the clerk arguing. He ran back to the truck to get his radio. Dad chased him, but Bud got to the truck first and kicked Dad in the chest, knocking him backwards. Bud closed the door and was about to call for help. I...I had no choice. I took out my gun and shot him in the head. He...um, he was shocked and he froze in place when he saw me pointing my gun at him."

Winona paused and shook her head, staring off into the distance. "There's not a night that goes by that I don't see his face. The shock...the fear he felt when he realized what was happening. I had never killed a person before. It was horrible. It haunts me constantly."

"I'm so sorry," Leah said, trying to sound sympathetic. "What'd you do next?"

"Well, Dad said we should go ahead with the plan—that we had gone too far to back out," she explained. "So, I gave my gun to Jimmy so he could shoot the clerk. We had to finish her at that point, you understand? Things had gone too far and it was Jimmy's fault. Afterward, I traded guns with Bud. We had the same kind, so it was an easy fix. That's when I let Jimmy beat up on me. I actually passed out at one point. When I came to, Dad was yelling at Jimmy that he almost killed me. Jimmy said he had to make it look real if we wanted to fool the cops. Dad told him to get his ass in the truck and then he came over to me and wanted to take me to the hospital. I was in pain, but I didn't feel like it was serious, so I told him to go and finish it. But after he left, I really thought I was going to die."

There was a long silence between the two of them. When Winona seemed to get control of her sobbing, Leah asked, "Why'd they bury the money with the body and leave it in the ground for so long?"

"It was only Dad who buried the money and Bud's body. We didn't trust that Jimmy would be able to wait that long to get his cut, so we didn't tell him where it was buried."

"Why Louisiana?"

"I dated a guy from Mechant Loup whose family had a piece of property in the middle of the swamps. It was as far away from Utah as we could find, and I knew no one would ever go digging around in those swamps. It was filled with alligators and snakes and there wasn't a building near it. It was even hard to walk around in. It was the perfect spot." She shook her head again. "We were so close, and then Jimmy had to go and screw things up again."

"But why leave the money in the ground for so long?" Leah pressed gently. "I mean, after all you had to go through to get it, why just bury it and leave it? Why not use it to improve your quality of life?"

"Thirty years is what I decided on," Winona explained. "It would be long enough that the authorities would forget about the case. It wouldn't be suspicious when I quit the company, because it would be time for my retirement anyway. So, basically, it was our retirement fund. All we had to do was work as normal people for the next thirty years and then retire from our jobs. You'd be surprised how easy it is to work a nine-to-five making peanuts when you know you've got a fortune waiting for you."

Winona paused for a moment and took a long breath. She had stopped crying, but there was still a sad look in her eyes as she continued her story. "The plan was for us to divvy up the cash three ways and use it a little at a time for the rest of our lives, so as not to bring suspicion upon ourselves."

"What happened with the boy from Louisiana? Why'd Jimmy kill him?"

"He was at the wrong place at the wrong time." Winona frowned. "I really wish he hadn't done that. He could've scared the kid away and he and Dad could've just come back home."

"But what happened?"

"Jimmy and Dad had dug up the money and carried most of it to the truck," Winona explained. "They were coming back for the last bag and to bury Bud again when they heard someone moving around in the woods. Jimmy snuck up and saw the boy take the satchel of money. That's when he grabbed the shovel and hit the boy in the head. Jimmy said he hid the shovel where they'll never find it. He also told Dad he didn't mean to hit the kid so hard, but I don't believe him. He's mean."

"Oh, they found the shovel."

Winona lifted an eyebrow. "Really?"

"Yep. The detectives from Louisiana believe it was taken from your boyfriend's barn."

"Yeah, I told them where to find it. Dad and Jimmy didn't want to get caught with digging tools."

There was a long pause where both women were silent.

"I still can't believe what you're telling me," Leah said, shaking her head. She was still squatting in the garden, frozen under the weight of Winona's revelations. "Why would you agree to go along with this?"

"Without that money, I knew there was no way I could ever give my daughters the life they deserved, and their father certainly doesn't give a shit about them. They've taken out loans for college. They both have car notes. They can't even afford to buy a house because their rent is so high. They're drowning in debt—just like I was and just like I knew they would be. Back then, I knew this was the only way I could ever hope to help them get a leg up in life. Sure, I had to wait thirty years to realize those dreams, but I knew it would be worth it in the end. It gave me hope."

Leah scowled, still befuddled that she hadn't suspected Winona even once over the years. "Your last name is Munday—the same as your mom's married name. There's no connection between you and Duke Smith. If there was, I would've found it thirty years ago."

"There isn't any, which is the only way our plan worked. My stepdad adopted me when I was young, so I carried his name. It was without my consent, but I was too young to argue. Had you known Duke and Jimmy were family, you would've suspected them of being involved right away." Winona fixed Leah with a pointed stare. "Right?"

"I guess so," Leah acknowledged, noting that the muzzle of the revolver had dipped so much that it was now pointing at the ground. "What are we doing here, Winona? How are we getting out of this situation?"

"I'll split half the money with you," Winona said without

hesitation. "Now that Dad and Jimmy are gone, there's enough for you and me to retire in peace and prosperity. We can be happy for once and forever."

"It's all here?" Leah indicated the fresh mounds of dirt scattered throughout the garden.

"Yeah. I buried it here last night." The muzzle of Winona's gun shifted toward the garden. "You can see for yourself. Just let me leave with my half and don't tell anyone what you know. You can take your half and we can both retire in peace as very rich women."

"I'm not for sale, Winona." Leah stood slowly to her feet. "I can't let you leave—with or without the money."

Winona shifted the muzzle of the pistol back toward Leah. "You can't stop me."

Just then, tires screeched and headlights flooded the front of Winona's house, illuminating Winona and temporarily blinding her. She shielded her eyes, trying to see what was happening.

"Drop the gun or I'll shoot you where you stand!" called a commanding voice that Leah recognized. It was Clint Wolf, and it was his turn to save her life.

"Wait, don't shoot," Leah called, holding up her right hand. She wasn't one bit intimidated by the situation. "She won't pull the trigger."

"How do you know?" Winona asked.

"I never once doubted you—not in thirty years," Leah said softly. "I've been by your side through it all. I fought for you. I trusted you. Now, it's your turn to trust me. I'll continue to stick by you all the way to the end, but I have to be alive to do that. If you kill me, you'll be all alone. There'll be no one to fight for you."

"You'd continue fighting for me?" Winona asked cautiously. "Even after everything I've done?"

"I will."

"Why?"

"I don't believe you're a bad person," Leah explained. "You were just desperate. Well, there's no need to be desperate any longer."

"But I'll go to prison."

"It's better than the alternative."

Winona hesitated. She shifted her eyes to the blinding light and then back to Leah. Leah stepped forward and held out her hand.

"Let me help you," she pleaded. "I've been with you since the beginning. Let me be there for you to the end."

"But—"

"I can get you off on insanity," Leah whispered so only Winona could hear. "You'll be free in a year. Trust me—there's enough evidence in my file to convince any jury."

"Really?" Winona asked.

"Really."

"Why would you do that for me?"

"Because I always believe my victims."

Winona's shoulders slumped and she sighed heavily. Finally, she stepped off the porch and handed her gun to Leah. "Thank you so much. I knew I could always count on—"

As soon as the fingers of Leah's left hand were wrapped around the revolver, she let out a vicious punch with her right hand that caught Winona square on the chin, dropping her in a heap on the ground. Leah tossed the gun aside and flipped Winona to her stomach. She dropped all of her weight to Winona's back, forcing her lungs to expel violently. After handcuffing the woman, Leah jerked her to her feet and shoved her up against the chief's truck.

"But...but I trusted you!" Winona wailed, blood pouring from her mouth. "You lied to me!"

"You've lied to me for thirty years, you little bitch." Leah shoved her face in Winona's. "How's it feel?"

CHAPTER 47

Two weeks later...

I leaned back from my desk and rubbed my eyes with the fingers of my left hand, careful not to put any pressure on the bandage. While the flesh on my palm was healing nicely, it was still tender to the touch. I had been diagnosed with a second-degree rope burn and they said it might take a few weeks to heal completely. Unfortunately, all of the calluses I'd worked so hard to develop over the years had been ripped off in a second, and I'd to start working on them all over again.

I glanced at the time displayed at the bottom corner of my computer screen. It was five o'clock on a Friday and it was time to go home for the weekend. I had gotten off the phone with Detective Leah Anderson about fifteen minutes ago, and she had notified me that Winona Munday had been formally charged with the murder of Bud Walker and the armed robbery of the armored car. Winona had also been charged as a principal to the murder of the young clerk, Rebecca.

"And get this," Leah had announced excitedly, "the insurance company that covered the $2,000,000 loss during the heist has been out of business for twenty years and, since they were already made whole, the president of the armored car company decided to donate the recovered money to Bud's daughter. She'll never have to work another day in her life."

"It won't bring her dad back," I'd mumbled, "but it'll sure make her life a little easier."

"That, it will." Leah had then tried to again thank me for helping solve her case, but I just brushed her off and hung up the phone.

Now, I opened the box I'd received from FedEx earlier today. It was from the Windrift Police Department and it contained my Beretta 92FS pistol that had fallen over the cliff. I found myself holding my breath as I unwrapped it and checked it for damage and functionality.

"Huh, not bad," I said aloud. Other than a couple of scratches that added character to the frame, it seemed operable. I cleared off my desktop and broke it down, examining each part carefully. Everything was fine. I had always loved my Beretta pistol, but I now respected the hell out of its toughness.

After reassembling it, I shoved it in my waistband. I was just standing to leave when Amy strode into my office. There was that stomp of determination in her walk, so I knew I wasn't going anywhere for a while and sank back to my chair.

"What's up?"

"I just got the lab reports back from the evidence we submitted in Zeke's case."

I held out a hand, but she ignored it and plopped to the chair opposite me, keeping the reports.

"Zeke McKenzie could not be excluded as a major contributor to the blood on the shovel and the flashlight," she read, squinting over the report. "Jimmy Smith could not be excluded as a major contributor to DNA swabs taken from the shovel. The DNA swabs from the flashlight were inconclusive. Winona Munday could not be excluded as a major contributor to the DNA swabs taken from the revolver found in Bud Walker's holster. So, we can link the shovel to Jimmy and Zeke, thus proving Jimmy killed Zeke. We can also link Winona to the handgun that killed Rebecca and Bud. We know Winona killed Bud, but Jimmy killed Rebecca."

I nodded. "What about the ballistics report? Does it confirm Winona's statement?"

"Yep, they were able to confirm that the gun in Bud's holster fired the bullet that killed him. It also fired the bullets that killed Rebecca." Amy glanced up and mean-mugged me. "By the way, I'm still pissed that I didn't get to go to Utah."

"You can go next time." I leaned back in my chair and folded my hands behind my head. "I'm getting too old to make those long road trips anyway."

"Shut up." She blew a tuft of blonde hair out of her eyes and turned back to the lab report. "You just turned forty, and that's not old anymore. They say it's the new teen or something."

"Stop aging me," I said, laughing. "I won't be forty for four more years."

"Then stop saying you're old."

"What else do you have?"

"That's about it." She tossed the report on my desk. "The rest is pretty cut and dry."

She was right. In addition to what we already had, Leah had faxed me the firearms qualification records from the armored car company for Bud and Winona. As part of weapons qualification, the company recorded the serial numbers of each employee's weapon on their re-qualification sheet. When Leah had compared the serial number on Winona's re-qual sheet to the serial number on the revolver we found in Bud's holster, they matched.

Likewise, the serial number on Bud's re-qual sheet matched the serial number on the revolver Leah had snatched from Winona's hand on the night Winona was arrested. Since Winona had started working in the warehouse after the heist, she never qualified with her weapon again and no one noticed the discrepancy.

Earlier last week, the Windrift Police Department had held a press conference exonerating Bud Walker of all wrongdoing and had issued a public apology. Several of the national news channels had covered the press conference and I'd been able to watch it from home. Leah told me they had also met privately with Bud's family and apologized to them, as well.

"They were very gracious," Leah had said when she called to tell me. "We didn't deserve for them to be so nice about it."

She might've been right, but there were truly good people in the world who understood that not everything or everyone is perfect.

"I guess it's on to the next case," Amy said, standing to leave. As I stood with her, she asked if I'd heard from Red.

"Not since I made the notification." Red's demeanor had been extremely intense as I told him about what we'd learned in Utah. When I'd gotten to the part about Jimmy being kicked off the cliff by Leah, he had lunged forward and wrapped me in a giant bear hug, vowing to somehow repay her for avenging his son's murder.

I indicated Amy with a nod of my head. "What about you?"

"Yeah, I saw him earlier," she said. "He's still in pain, but I can tell he's not as angry anymore. He told me to tell you how thankful he was for your work. He said he was glad Jimmy Smith was dead."

I only nodded as I followed Amy down the hall and out into the afternoon sun.

Susan was in the gym trying to teach Grace to throw a push kick when I got home. They both turned to look when my shadow darkened the doorway, and Grace screeched when she saw me.

"Daddy!" She shot like a bullet toward the door, but as fast as her little legs were pumping, they were no match for Achilles and Coco, who reached me seconds before she did.

I scooped Grace up in my right arm while rubbing my dogs with my left hand. They licked aggressively at my hand, each trying to outdo the other.

Susan, who was dripping sweat, removed her punch mitts and began removing the wraps from her hands. I kissed her sweaty mouth and Grace screeched again.

"Oh-oh! Daddy kissing Mommy!"

"I was thinking we should go out to dinner tonight," Susan said, tickling Grace's stomach. "What about you, Pumpkin? Do you want to go eat out?"

"I want McDonalds!" Grace said, her red curls bouncing as she shook her head up and down. "I want French fries!"

Susan and I laughed.

"You can have French fries," Susan said, "but it won't be from McDonalds."

I followed Susan inside so we could change and I told her about the crime lab reports as we walked. When I was done, she told me that Gretchen had stopped by earlier.

"What'd she say?" I asked, anxious to know if there was something wrong with Achilles.

"She took Achilles to the back of the property, then they left in her truck and were gone for an hour or so." She shrugged. "When she brought him back, she said he was very healthy and very well-mannered." She turned and tickled Grace, taking her from my arms. "Unlike your Daddy—huh, Pumpkin?"

I scoffed and pounded my chest with a fist. "I'm very healthy, too."

"That's not the part I was talking about."

I only grunted. I was hungry and ready for a night out with my family. If there was one thing that murder cases did for me, it was that it deepened my appreciation for time spent with my family. Time was short. No one was guaranteed another breath, and I vowed to spend as much of it as I could with Susan and Grace.

"Maybe we can have a conversation after dinner," I mumbled casually as I ambled past Susan. "A *long* conversation."

BJ Bourg

BJ Bourg is an award-winning mystery writer and former professional boxer who hails from the swamps of Louisiana. Dubbed the "real deal" by other mystery writers, he has spent his entire adult life solving crimes as a patrol cop, detective sergeant, and chief investigator for a district attorney's office. Not only does he know his way around crime scenes, interrogations, and courtrooms, but he also served as a police sniper commander (earning the title of "Top Shooter" at an FBI sniper school) and a police academy instructor.

Bourg's debut novel, JAMES 516, won the 2016 EPIC eBook Award for Best Mystery, and BUT NOT FORGOTTEN was a finalist for the same award in 2017. Dozens of his articles and stories have been published in national magazines such as Woman's World, Boys' Life, and Writer's Digest. He is a regular contributor to two of the nation's leading law enforcement magazines, Law and Order and Tactical Response, and he has taught at conferences for law enforcement officers, tactical police officers, and writers. Above all else, he is a father and husband, and the highlight of his life is spending time with his beautiful wife and wonderful children.

http://www.bjbourg.com

Made in United States
Orlando, FL
07 January 2025

56993345R00118